How dare this arrogant creature, this reckless driver, this road hog imply she was a crook? When words finally came to her, she heard herself say, "I'm calling the police."

He gave a jeering laugh and looked at his watch again. "Do you have a phone in that priceless antique? You'd better take my offer, otherwise you might find yourself the one with increased insurance premiums. My plane leaves in forty-five minutes, and I plan to be on it. There hasn't been any bodily damage to either of us, and I doubt the repairs to the car even warrant calling the police. You have my name and number, lady. Just let me know where your wreck's being repaired, and I'll go down and make sure you're not trying to rook me."

"Don't you dare leave the scene of the crime!" she replied.

"Crime?" he asked through thin lips. "I haven't murdered anyone—yet."

Dear Reader,

Although our culture is always changing, the desire to love and be loved is a constant in every woman's heart. Silhouette Romances reflect that desire, sweeping you away with books that will make you laugh and cry, poignant stories that will move you time and time again.

This year we're featuring Romances with a playful twist. Remember those fun-loving heroines who always manage to get themselves into tricky predicaments? You'll enjoy reading about their escapades in Silhouette Romances by Brittany Young, Debbie Macomber, Annette Broadrick and Rita Rainville.

We're also publishing Romances by many of your all-time favorites such as Ginna Gray, Diana Palmer and Joan Hohl. Your overwhelming reaction to these authors has served as a touchstone for us, and we're pleased to bring you more books with Silhouette's distinctive medley of charm, wit and—above all—*romance*. I hope you enjoy this book, and the many stories to come.

Sincerely,

Rosalind Noonan
Senior Editor
SILHOUETTE BOOKS

JOAN SMITH
The Infamous Madam X

Silhouette *Romance*

Published by Silhouette Books New York

America's Publisher of Contemporary Romance

SILHOUETTE BOOKS
300 East 42nd St., New York, N.Y.   10017

ISBN: 0-373-08430-7

First Silhouette Books printing May 1986

America's Publisher of Contemporary Romance

Printed in the U.S.A.

JOAN SMITH

has written many Regency romances, but likes working with the greater freedom of contemporaries. She also enjoys mysteries and Gothics, collects Japanese porcelain and is a passionate gardener. A native of Canada, she is the mother of three.

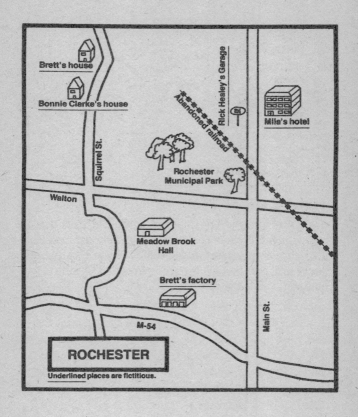

Brett's house

Bonnie Clarke's house

Squirrel St.

Rick Healey's Garage

Abandoned railroad

Mila's hotel

Rochester
Municipal Park

Walton

Meadow Brook
Hall

Brett's factory

Main St.

M-54

ROCHESTER

Underlined places are fictitious.

Chapter One

The big black limousine cruised along at fifty-five mph with a luxurious purr from the powerful engine. It felt like driving a bus. Mila was sorry she had to drive Madam X at night, but if Rick was going to prep her for the show, she had to get the car into his garage not later than eight tomorrow morning. It was kind of Rick to phone and offer his mechanical expertise. Never having shown Madam X before, Mila hadn't realized this was necessary, but it sounded like a good idea to have a mechanic go over it.

When you're trying to sell a classic car worth a couple of hundred thousand dollars, you want it to be in top shape. Rochester, Michigan, where the Meadow Brook Concours d'Élégance classic car show took place, was one hundred fifty miles from Muskegon, and it was either leave home at four-thirty in the morning or drive for an hour in the dark tonight. Mila preferred to be there in plenty of time.

At least there wasn't much traffic. She'd passed through a few foggy patches that worried her, but she was clear of them now. Of course the one hundred percent safe thing to do would have been to have the car delivered on the back of a truck. Unfortunately, the safe thing cost money, two hundred fifty bucks to be exact.

A smile curved Mila's lips as she sailed along through the dark night. Soon money worries would be a thing of the past. Dad hadn't left her mother much life insurance and his prolonged illness and funeral had eaten up most of their savings. But he'd left her Madam X, a limited-edition 1932 Imperial Cadillac in perfectly restored condition. Dad had been the classic car enthusiast of the family. He'd bought Madam X years ago for fifteen hundred dollars, and lovingly restored her in his garage when he wasn't fixing other people's engines. His hobby, he called it. His wife called the car less innocent names—she considered it the other woman in her husband's life. Over the years, Mrs. Dempster had developed a lively distaste for Madam X.

It was understood that the car was the family's life insurance policy. Mila wondered how much it would bring. Only 391 of them were ever produced, between 1930 and 1933, so that only a handful survived. The last one shown had sold for nearly two hundred thousand dollars five years ago, and the price would be

even higher now. More than enough to ensure that
Mom didn't have to sell the house, and that Bobbie
could go to college.

As for Mila, she could support herself. A public
school teacher didn't make a bundle, but she made a
good living wage, and the "psychic income," or personal satisfaction of working with the kids was great.
With a bit of careful budgeting, she should be able to
afford her own four-wheeled luxury in a few years. A
Boss Mustang was what she considered a car. Both she
and Bobbie were into sixties' muscle cars.

Mila's jaws clenched in anxiety when a light mist
began to cloud the windshield and coat the road with
a slippery film. Madam X's tires weren't exactly the
latest radial wonders. She even considered parking
until the light rain stopped, but this stretch of road
didn't have broad shoulders. She was only ten miles
from Rochester so she decided to just slow down and
continue, very carefully. A valley lay before her, cur-
tained in wisps of floating fog, but visibility was still
fair. She slowed to forty, then to thirty when she saw
the Curve Ahead sign. A sudden lightening of the
shadows on her left, a pale reflection of oncoming
headlights around the curve, caused her heart to
pound. She pulled well to the right and eased forward, hugging the shoulder, but her car was large, and
the road was narrow.

Mila had about a second and a half to realize she
was going to be hit by the approaching car that had
crossed the center line in a carelessly wide turn. The
driver made a belated effort to pull over, but at his

speed it only threw the car into a skid on the slick
pavement. She saw the blinding glare of two bright
headlights zooming at her through the fog. Her heart
felt as if it had stopped beating and she thought, My
God, I'm going to be killed! Instinctively her foot
rammed on the brake. When she heard the squeal of
tires, the sickening rip of metal, when she felt the jar
of collision and the hard edge of the steering wheel
rammed against her chest, she had the unsatisfying
consolation of knowing it wasn't her fault. Then she
passed out, not from injury but from shock.

The world went completely pitch-black for about
thirty seconds. As if from a long distance, Mila heard
her motor still running. Before she even opened her
eyes, she reached out and turned off the ignition.
Without realizing it, she was putting the care of
Madam X before her own safety. The blackness re-
ceded and she shook away the scary feeling of dis-
orientation that came from being alone on a foggy
night on an unfamiliar road. Why was it so bright?
The lights! She'd turned off the engine and left the
headlights burning—she'd wear out the battery. She
pushed in the light button and leaned back against the
seat to collect her wits and thank God that she had
survived intact.

At least she thought she was in one piece. Nothing
hurt. She carefully moved her neck, her arms and her
legs, one at a time. Breathing didn't hurt, so her chest
and lungs had escaped harm. She looked down at her
hands for signs of blood. Her trembling fingers were
clean. Just recovering from the shock, she only then

realized that it was still bright enough to see all this. The other car's headlights were shining in the windshield of Madam X.

Mila felt a wild spasm of fear that the other driver might be hurt, even dead, though the car wasn't that badly damaged. Only a fender bender, from what she could see.

Only a fender bender! The car show was just three days away, and these old classic cars were almost impossible to get parts for. It would never be fixed in three days, and that meant waiting another whole year for the next show. You attracted a wider field of buyers and got a much better price if you had a show ribbon to go with the car. All the collectors were gathered there at the show, and a sale was almost assured. It could mean thousands of dollars' difference. She was afraid to get out and look, but steeled herself for the thoroughly unpleasant duty.

These thoughts flew through Mila's mind in seconds as she reached for the door handle. There were signs of life in the other car, too. The door opened and a tall man slowly got out, testing his limbs before he straightened up. His headlights were behind him as he came toward her. All she saw was his outline—a tall, slender but wide-shouldered man, wearing a light suit. His head was bent forward. She opened her door and went to meet him halfway. Now she could see he was young, though somewhat older than her own twenty-three years. He looked thirtyish, he had dark hair and was wearing a scowl.

"Are you hurt?" he asked. His voice was sharp with concern.

"I guess not. Are you okay?"

"No, I am *not* okay," he answered angrily, and turned back to examine his car.

Mila did the same with hers. The black car was harder to see than the man's silver one. It was nearly swallowed up in shadow and the rain, which was coming down harder now. The body was splashed with mud, robbing Madam X of her sheen. Mila felt sick with regret to see the left-front fender crumpled. Its metal was too thick to be pushed in like an accordion, as the man's car was, but it was severely damaged. The left headlight, a heavy, chrome-plated parabola that stood up on a chrome bar, was knocked askew. From the corner of her eye she noticed the man had bent down and was running his fingers over the dented fender of his shiny sports car, while an angry mutter that sounded extremely profane issued from his lips.

After a moment he rose and turned back to her, glaring. "My brand new Porsche," he said bitterly, as though it were *her* fault. "I haven't had it a month. Look at the bumper, cut to ribbons. What the hell are you driving, a Mack truck? That behemoth takes up three-quarters of the road."

"It's your fault!" she charged.

"It's nobody's fault. It was an accident." He looked at his watch, then back at his car, shaking his head angrily. "Look, I'm in a hurry. I have to catch a plane. There doesn't seem to be much damage here—a fender bender. What do you day we—"

"Not much damage!" she objected. "I'll never be able to get this car fixed."

He came forward and leaned over her twisted fender. The lights played on a ruggedly handsome face and a shock of dark hair falling forward. His cheeks were lean, and about his mouth she saw a touch of arrogance.

"I don't know why you kids drive these old wrecks," he said dismissively. "You can see by the position of our cars that this was a no-fault accident. We're both on the line, so we'll blame it on the weather."

"You were driving like a lunatic! It's *your* fault."

"Look at our wheels," he pointed out.

It was true neither set of wheels passed the center line now, but hers were farther within the safe boundaries. "My car pushed yours back," she said. "You were over the line."

"That's possible. I went into a skid because of the rain—I was in a hurry. I still am. I'd prefer to settle this without the help of the police and insurance boys. I'll accept the responsibility. Here's my card," he said, rifling in his pocket and handing her a business card. "I'm leaving for New York immediately. I'll be back tomorrow afternoon. Get a price on your repairs and I'll pay the bill."

She glanced at the card without seeing. "But you don't understand. This is Madam X," she said.

His eyes narrowed. "What have you been smoking?" he growled. "Damned students."

She was furious at this charge. "I haven't been smoking anything! My car's a priceless antique."

"Sure, and my Porsche cost a million dollars. Funny the way cars' values escalate once there's been an accident. Quite certain you aren't suffering whiplash, too? That's where the real money is. If I had time, I'd insist you go to the hospital now and be checked out, and by God, I *would* call the cops. Don't think you'll be taking me to the cleaners, just because my card says Halbrett Fletcher."

Her mouth flew open at this new slur on her character. She was so incensed she couldn't think of anything to say. How dare this arrogant creature, this reckless driver, this road hog imply she was a crook? When words finally came to her, she heard herself say, "I'm calling the police."

He gave a jeering laugh, and looked at his watch again. "Do you have a car phone in that priceless antique? You'd better take my offer, otherwise you might find yourself the one with increased insurance premiums. My plane leaves in forty-five minutes, and I plan to be on it. There hasn't been any bodily damage to either of us, and I doubt the repairs to the car even warrant calling the police. You have my name and number, lady. Just notify me where your wreck's being repaired, and I'll go down and make sure you're not trying to rook me."

"Don't you dare leave the scene of the crime!" she replied.

"Crime?" he asked, through thin lips. "I haven't murdered anyone—yet."

He turned on his heel and stalked to his car. While he opened the door and turned the key, the echo of her threats hung on the air. "...leaving the scene of an accident...hit and run..." and a lot of other phrases meant to intimidate him.

He opened his window and called, "You've got my card. You know where to find me, Madam X." Then he gunned the gas, backed off and continued on his way at a slightly reduced pace, but in a thoroughly bad mood. "Priceless antique" indeed! he thought. A twisted old hulk of metal that should have been scrapped decades ago. And being driven by some hopped-up teenager who probably didn't even have a license. If he hadn't opened his door against that Lincoln in the parking lot just a month ago, he would have called the insurance agent, but a second incident would probably raise his rates through the roof. The repairs to the old wreck shouldn't be more than a hundred—maybe two.

Whatever he had to pay, it was better than missing his meeting in New York. It would look extremely derelict if the president of the board was late for the annual shareholders' meeting of Fletcher Enterprises. Did the kid recognize his name? Was that why her old tin lizzy was suddenly a priceless antique? The name of Fletcher was pretty well known around these parts, of course. Fletcher Ball Bearings, Fletcher Surgical Instruments, Fletcher Metal Molding. And if the shareholders went along with it, Fletcher Casting Works would be next.

The kid didn't look like the street-smart type. She was sort of dazed looking. Maybe he'd have his lawyer look her up before he got back from New York. Idiot! He hadn't even got her name or license number, and obviously Madam X wouldn't be her listing in the phone book. Why did she call herself that? Well, she had his card, and he could certainly look forward to hearing from her, or her lawyer. This settled, he reverted to thoughts of business while he sped toward the airport.

Back at the scene of the accident, Mila stood fuming impotently in the middle of the road, without even realizing the rain was increasing. When it began to soak through her jacket, she got back in the car and just sat, shaking from cold, anger and regret. Five minutes later, she tried the engine. It worked fine. The left headlight's beam shot off at a crazy angle that made her car look walleyed, but she couldn't do anything about that.

She drove till she reached the outskirts of Rochester, and stopped at a reasonably priced motel. The Home-away-from-Home, it was called. She got a cup of coffee in the coffee shop and took it to her unit. It was no home, but a dreary, standard cheap motel room, with garishly flowered wallpaper and a red corduroy bedspread. The cheerful colors only depressed her more. She looked at the phone, knowing she should call her mother and tell her the grim news. Why do it before morning? Let her mother get a night's sleep, even if she'd be awake half the night herself.

She stood looking through the rain-splattered window at Madam X, parked right outside, and sipped her coffee. Tomorrow she'd phone Rick Healey at his garage and see if he could do anything, but she knew how slim the chance was. You didn't just blithely order new parts for a car that was more than fifty years old. It was a question of scrounging around, looking for someone with an Imperial Cadillac too far gone to be restored, who was willing to sell off a precious piece for any price he cared to ask. To have a reproduction made would lower the value of the car. And you didn't find parts in three days.

Of course insurance companies didn't care to insure cars like that, except for public liability and property damage. If that man—Halbrett something—didn't do as he'd promised and pay for the repairs, she'd never get Madam X back in top show condition. Oh, why hadn't she paid the truckers the two hundred fifty dollars to haul the car safely? For a measly two hundred fifty dollars she'd risked a thousand times that. That was the kind of price Madam X could bring in. But whoever would have thought she, who had never had an accident in her life, would have one tonight, during a short drive along little-used roads, in weather that had been perfectly clear when she left? Besides, she'd wanted that one last, farewell drive in the classic car.

Mila thought of the many times her dad had piled the family in for a picnic or drive on Sundays, while he was fixing the car up. The first few times people had only looked and smiled in amusement. Then as the car approached completion, the amusement had turned to admiration. Crowds would gather around, asking questions, praising it. How her father's chest had swelled in pride and joy. Then the past few years, Madam X became much too valuable to be driven for pleasure. Mila now felt almost as bad as if she'd injured her father, instead of only a car.

And it was all that man's fault—Hal Brett something. Or had he said Hall Brett? A sharp image of him was etched in her mind. The arrogant, angry face, with those lean cheeks and deep-set eyes. The sneering insults, the insinuation that she meant to gouge him. It just showed the way his mind worked. He was so ignorant he hadn't recognized a classic car when he saw one. Of course in the fog and dark and rain... Really she didn't have much idea what his car was like, either.

She went to put her jacket on a hanger to dry, and rooted in the pocket for the man's card. She took it out and read Avery Malcolm, D.D.S., and the address in Rochester. He'd given her somebody else's card! He didn't mean to pay at all. She'd let him get away, and didn't know a thing about him except that he *said* his name was Halbrett something, and that he'd be driving a Porsche with a dented fender.

He wouldn't get away with it. She'd go to every Porsche dealer in the vicinity. She'd hound him like Nemesis, until he'd wish he'd never left the scene of the accident. She'd... Her courage failed, and she sat slumped on the corner of the bed with warm tears trickling down her cheeks. She shivered and pulled the red corduroy bedspread around her shoulders, trying to dissipate the chill that came from within. It was the chill of remorse, and despair. She'd *never* find him. Madam X would never be perfect again, never bring the fortune she was supposed to.

After a bout of tears, Mila decided to take a hot shower to get rid of the chill. She went to the bathroom and looked in the mirror. How horrible she looked, with her tawny red hair turned to dark brown by rain, plastered against her head. Her face had turned white, and her eyes were red from crying. She looked all of sixteen. A very frightened sixteen. The man thought she was some dumb kid whom he could pull a fast trick on, but she'd show him.

Chapter Two

"Jeez, Mila, you dented Madam X!" Rick Healey exclaimed when she drove the car into his garage the next morning at eight. "How'd you do that? Oh, boy, she's a goner," he said, walking all around the limousine and shaking his curly brown head.

Rick was one of the fortunate few who had known what he wanted to do with his life from the time he could walk. His only toys had been cars, his only hobby fiddling around with them. Though he was now just twenty-six, he was already vastly experienced. Five years before he had heard rumors of an exotic car in the state. He'd driven to Muskegon, knocked on the door, introduced himself and respectfully asked for permission to see Madam X. It was the beginning of a courtship that continued uninterrupted over the years.

Rick liked all cars, but preferred older vehicles. Anything under forty was not what he'd call a real car. Circumstances forced him to keep steady company with a '71 Barracuda—a mere teenager, but with special qualities that he was more than willing to extol to anyone who'd listen. She was only a plaything, to be used for drag racing if he ever got her tuned up. Meanwhile he made his living working on other people's cars.

The hauling about of wheels and engines had developed a bulging set of muscles on Rick's six-foot frame. Enthusiasm lent a glow to his friendly brown eyes. Apart from his way of making chopped liver of the English language, Mila liked him. Today she noticed he wasn't wearing his usual coveralls but a gaudy T-shirt and jeans. It was a promotional T-shirt with Healey Does It With Oil printed on the back. The shirt was yellow, the words black, and a red oilcan sprinkled red streaks of oil over the whole.

"Boy, you really trashed her," he said, shaking his head in sorrow. His big, capable hands ran lovingly over the twisted metal that held on the headlight. "What happened?"

She explained the accident. "Do you think it's possible to get it fixed up before the show?" she asked.

"Before the show?" he asked, brown eyes blinking in astonishment. "Mila, baby, why don't you just ask me for the moon? It takes months, even years, hunting down parts. You remember how long it took me and Doug to find the radiator? We had to have it shipped from California.'' Doug, of course, was Mila's father.

"Out of the question to fix this one, huh?'' she said, resigned. She had already known it.

"Afraid so, doll. I'm devastated—really, totally. That ain't no way to treat a lady.'' Rick referred to cars and women in loving and interchangeable terms. Sometimes it was hard to know just which he was talking about. "Of course, I'll give it my best shot. I'll take the fender off and see if I can hammer the bend out. Meanwhile I'll put this baby in the back of the shop. We don't want her out where guys can get their hands on her. What beauty—awesome.'' He patted Madam X's fender as he spoke. "I might be able to straighten out the chrome bar that holds on the head-lights. It'd have to be rechromed though. It couldn't be done for this year's show. Maybe next year . . .''

"Yeah, maybe next year,'' she said, blinking back a tear.

"What you got to do is get after the guy that hit the car. You can take him for plenty. What'd you say his name is again?''

"I don't know. Halbrett something, he said. Or maybe it was Hal Brett.''

"Well, as long as you have his license number.''

"I don't.''

Rick turned a disbelieving eye on her. "What do you mean? You didn't let the creep drive away with-out getting some ID? Are you nuts or what?''

"He gave me a card, but it's not his. At least I don't think it is.'' She handed it to Rick.

"I know Doc Malcolm. He replaced a filling for me a month ago. Nice old guy, gray hair, but mean! He nearly fractured my jaw."

She shook her head. "No, that's not him. Malcolm must be his dentist, I suppose, since he had his card."

"What kind of a car did the guy drive?"

"A Porsche."

"There aren't too many of those in town. Maybe I know him."

"This was a new car. He said it was only a month old."

"I'll call around and see if I can get a line on him—Mr. X. Young guy, you said, tall, dark-haired?"

"That's right." But the vague description didn't seem to fully describe the man, who was fast becoming an obsession with Mila.

She shook away the memory of his searing insults. "About the car, Rick. That man in California who sold Dad the radiator—does he still have his Cadillac available for parts? He might happen to have a left-front fender. Will you give him a call?"

"Sure, doll face. I'll get right on it. Pity it couldn't be ready for this year. Madam X has been advertised as one of the major attractions of the show. They put her picture in the brochure and everything. There's going to be a lot of frustrated guys coming all the way from Texas and Toronto to bid. Oh well, the price'll only go up next year. Might as well look on the bright side."

"What do you figure the man will ask for the fender?"

"Anything he wants. An arm and a leg and four eyeteeth. Something like that."

"What would that be in dollars?"

He hunched his shoulders. "Five hundred—more like five thousand—anything the market will bear. I mean when there's only one or two of a thing available in the whole world..."

Her heart sank. "Five thousand," she whispered incredulously.

"There's gold in them there parts. Want me to give him a buzz?"

"Uh, well, yes, but do you think he'd accept installment payments?"

"Nah. You'll have to get a loan at the bank. Hey, you're a school teacher, doll. No sweat. Or your mom could mortgage the house."

A blinding red rage surged up in Mila's head. Her mother would actually have to mortgage the family home because that creature drove like a lunatic, and sneaked away without leaving his real name. Her own foolish behavior was just as bad. But how was a person supposed to have her wits about her when she'd just come within an inch of being killed? "Yes, sure," she said bitterly. "Mom can just mortgage the house."

"Are you sticking around town for the show?"

"I'd planned to go home and come back with Mom and Bobbie. I'll stay a day though, to try to locate the—*person* who wrecked Madam X."

"Where are you putting up?"

"I'm at the Home-away-from-Home Motel."

"You'll need wheels. That's way the hell out of town. Why don't you switch to something closer? Maybe we can have lunch together. Meanwhile, you can borrow a car. Not my Barracuda. I've got a sweetheart of a Boss 302 Mustang in the garage. What a doll! She's insured for test drives, so it's okay, but drive carefully. Hey, you didn't compliment me on my new shirts. Want one? They cost five bucks."

It wasn't the price, but revulsion at the sleazy magnificence of the printing that caused her to demur.

"Everybody's doing it," he urged. "You know, like Plumbers Do It with a Wrench. Piano Players Do It with—"

"I know, Rick. But school teachers have to do it with class," she joked.

"I've got two hundred of them to sell."

He took Mila to show her a flashy white Boss Mustang, all polished and gleaming and looking like new. Mila's eyes gleamed as brightly as the paint when she saw it. "Wow! How much are you asking for this?"

"A lot. She's in A-1 restored condition. All original parts. No repros. Hood scoop, louvers, mag 500's, spoiler." He pointed out these features as he spoke.

Mila took the keys and started the engine. It rumbled with a steady beat as pistons flew up and down. Driving that car was the only enjoyable moment of her day. It was like flying. She checked out of the motel and drove back to town, riding up and down the streets until she found a respectable small hotel with rates she was comfortable with. It ran through her mind that the car she was driving probably wouldn't cost much more than the fender she had to replace.

At noon she went back to the garage, where Rick was just washing grease from his hands before lunch. "Did you reach the man in California?" she asked.

"Henderson wasn't in. I'm calling back this afternoon. I have a few other possible sources, too. How about a hamburger?" he asked.

"Sounds good."

Over lunch, he reported on his search for the man he called Mr. X. "I called Doc Malcolm. He doesn't have a whole lot of patients that drive Porsches. There's a lady who drives one—it could be her husband. He's tall and dark. And there's Brett Fletcher. I thought he'd been driving a white Corvette all along. I didn't hear he bought a Porsche."

"That's him! That's the name. Halbrett Fletcher," she said eagerly.

"His name's Brett. Could be a nickname, I guess. Oh, boy! You would have to tangle with Mr. A-1 Big Shot. There's no way you'll win a case against *him*. He practically owns the town. Half the lawyers work for him. He knows senators and mayors, judges—people like that," he said, with a meaningful lift of his brow.

"Where does he live?"

"I looked him up in the phone book. He's not listed, but his factories are in the industrial park, just above M-59. Fletcher Enterprises. Want to give him a call?"

"Yes," she said, quickly striding to the phone.

"I'd like to speak to Mr. Fletcher, please," she said, when a polite female voice answered.

"I'm sorry, Mr. Fletcher is out of town. He's expected back late this afternoon. Would you like to leave a message?"

Mila's name would mean nothing to him. She used what he, in his gross ignorance, seemed to think was her name. "Yes, you can tell him Madam X phoned, and will be in touch with him."

"Madam X?" the woman asked.

"That's right. The woman whose car he hit last night. I'm calling about his leaving the scene of an accident. You can tell him he underestimated the damage. Five thousand dollars is the price my mechanic mentioned. You'll be sure to tell him I called?"

"Yes, ma'am," the woman said in alarm.

"Thank you." She hung up and stomped back to the table.

"You look like a bulldog, Mila," Rick said. "I'd use a little tact on Fletcher if I were you. He has a weakness for ladies. If you bat your eyes at him, he might cough up for the repairs."

"He'll pay all right. It was his fault."

"You'll never prove it now. What you should've done was stay there, and call the cops."

"Oh, sure, I should have left a quarter of a million dollars sitting in the road for the next lousy driver to really demolish while I plodded along a dark road in the rain. That would've been clever. He'd already left, and there wasn't a house in sight."

Rick considered this and indicated by a shrug of his shoulders that she might have a point. "I've got to get back to work. Want to come along?"

"No, I have to phone Mom and tell her the news."

"That won't take long."

"That's what you think. It'll take a couple of hours to screw up my courage, and another couple of hours to recuperate. I think I'll have a nap after. I'm bushed."

"Yeah, you look rotten."

"Thanks, Rick."

"Sorry, doll face. Tired, red eyes, bags under them—that's all I meant."

"Oh, is that all? For a minute there I was afraid I didn't look my usual gorgeous self," she said ironically.

"I was thinking about Fletcher. What you should do is go to his office all fixed up nice. Wear makeup, perfume, high heels, slinky dress."

"Black undies, garter belt? That type, is he?"

Rick smiled approvingly. "Yeah, he has the most *amazing* women, Mila. He goes around with this girl—jeez, you should see her. She drives a Clenet. Imagine! They cost a fortune. And I saw him once with a woman in a Rolls-Royce Corniche. At least I think it was Fletcher. She was something. Boy, talk about streamlined. What a chassis. A silver dream."

"The woman?"

"No, the Rolls!"

"Oh."

In the restaurant, Mila noticed a few T-shirts that said Fletcher Team Mate, and pointed them out to Rick. "Baseball team," he said. "You see them all over town. Fletcher sponsors the Rochester Rockets."

After lunch, Mila went to her hotel and braced herself for the call home. Her mother was every bit as upset as expected.

"Oh, Mila! Not an accident. I knew no good would ever come from that darned car. Are you all right, honey?"

"I'm fine."

"And . . . the car?" her mother asked fearfully.

"The jerk who hit me is trying to get off without paying, but I'm going to stay over a day and go after him."

"The scoundrel! Who is he?"

"Brett Fletcher, and he's worse than a scoundrel. He's an arrogant jackass who practically owns the town, according to Rick."

"Oh, my!" her mother exclaimed, surprised at such language from Mila. "He sounds kind of dangerous."

"It's not too bad," Mila said, softening the blow as much as possible when she told the story. "Anyway, the man will have to pay."

"So we'll have to wait another year to sell," her mother said resignedly. "Well, if we have to, we have to. Don't blame yourself. I can always get a small mortgage on the house, and pay it off when we sell Madam X. I have Daddy's little pension, you know, and you have a good job, so we'll get by."

A lump rose in Mila's throat. She would almost have preferred her mother to blame her, instead of trying to console her. "I should have had the car delivered on a truck," she said.

"Don't blame yourself, dear. You were only trying to save me money. And you're a good, safe driver. I'm sure it wasn't your fault."

"I'm sorry, Mom."

"It's all right. As long as you weren't hurt, that's the main thing."

But she was hurt. A deep, dull ache gnawed at her innards, and her heart felt actually physically sore. She drew the drapes and lay down to rest. Some peace was possible now that she'd confessed the truth to her mother. Fatigued from a sleepless night, she soon dozed off into a fitful nap. When she opened her eyes, it was three o'clock, and she phoned Mr. Fletcher again.

"He came in, but wanted to go home to change and shower," his secretary said. "I gave him your message, er, Madam X. He was very upset. He said if you call again to get a number where he can reach you. He'll be back soon."

Mila looked at the phone and gave the number. She felt a little smug satisfaction that he was "very upset." As she lay daydreaming, she remembered Rick's reading of the man's character. A rich playboy, apparently. Fond of fast cars and fast women. Yes, she could picture that arrogant face amidst a bevy of beautiful females, those dark eyes smoldering in passion. His hands with those long, sculptured fingers stroking her flesh. *Her* flesh? A shiver scuttled along her spine. She shook the thought away. She supposed he'd be considered handsome, if he ever stopped scowling and cursing.

But handsome or ugly, he was the cause of that accident, and she wouldn't rig herself out in any slinky gown and perfume to seduce him into doing the right thing. The very memory of him was so upsetting that sleep was impossible. Mila opened the drapes and saw the sun shining. The room felt muggy, and she decided to have a quick dip in the hotel pool to refresh herself.

She'd packed a bathing suit, and fished it out of her suitcase. Mila wasn't one of those dry bathers who put on a wisp of bikini to decorate the pool edge. She wiggled into a one-piece green suit that emphasized her green eyes. They were wide-set, and dominated her fine-boned face. The suit plunged low in front, revealing the beginning curve of her bosom, but it had good solid straps for serious swimming. Her body was small and well proportioned, with high, firm breasts and a tiny waist. The cut of the suit made her legs look long and emphasized the feminine flare of her hips. In the humid air her naturally curly hair had turned to a tousle of wisps and tendrils. It feathered over her forehead and played against her cheeks. It was long at the back so she could wear it up when she was teaching and look intimidating, but out of school it hung loose. The sun slanting through the window picked out its tawny orange-gold highlights, making a halo around her face.

She got her keys and sunglasses, and with a quick glance in the mirror, she picked up a hotel towel and went out. A stop at the desk was necessary, to tell them she was expecting a call and would take it at the pool-side.

She selected a table away from the other bathers and arranged herself comfortably, putting on her dark glasses and leaning back in the lounge chair to soak up the sun. When the waiter came around, she ordered a pineapple juice. No one would guess to see her so in-dolent in the middle of a workday afternoon that she was anything but a well-heeled tourist enjoying her-self. One of the chief benefits of being a teacher was that her summers were free, and now, in August, she had already made use of it to work on a golden tan.

Mila looked so different from the night before that Brett Fletcher didn't even recognize her when he fi-nally traced the number she'd left and followed it to the hotel. He had vainly searched the parking lot, hoping to assess the damage to her car himself. That threatening mention of a ridiculous five thousand dollars had set his blood boiling. Blackmail was the word that came to mind. Not knowing her name, he'd scanned the register for single women who had booked in the night before. Finding none, he had learned from the clerk that a young woman had come in that morning and was at the pool. His dark eyes passed over Mila, searching for a brash teenager. When he ascertained no such person was present, he took a second, interested look at what he mentally called the "cute little redhead." She was built like a wasp, with a waist he could encircle with his two hands.

The kid wasn't here, but looking for her made a good excuse to introduce himself to the redhead. He strolled forward and stopped in front of Mila's lounge chair. A smile curved his thin lips as he gazed at that flaming halo of red curls. Her dark glasses concealed any familiarity that might have told him who she was, and as she had closed her eyes, she didn't see him. He made a leisurely survey of her charms, spread out below him, before speaking. Some sixth sense told her she was no longer alone. When she opened her eyes, Brett was making a detailed examination of her breasts.

She recognized that haughty face at once, and the very sight of it filled her with violence. She could read lechery and the decadence of a spoiled rich man in every line of his proud body. Wouldn't you know he'd be wearing an expensive suit that looked hand-stitched around the lapels? Her body went perfectly rigid. She jerked to a sitting position and said, "So you came!"

First his smile withered, then it turned to a cold sneer. "Madam X, I presume?"

"Mr. Fletcher—or are you being Dr. Malcolm today?"

He looked at her in confusion. "What are you talking about?"

She lifted her chin pugnaciously. "About your little stunt of giving me a phony card, just before you cavalierly fled the scene of the accident."

"I told you my name!" he charged angrily. "As to that accident—if you think you're going to bleed me for five thousand bucks, lady, you're crazy. Where did you hide the car?"

These charges got her up from the chair in fury, and it was very annoying that she still had to look up at him. "Hide it?" she howled. "I didn't hide it. I took it to Rick Healey's Garage. The damages might go even higher—maybe twice as high," she said wildly. "It all depends on whether he can fix the rest of it or not."

His nostrils pinched, and his eyes narrowed to slits. "I begin to understand how you can afford to wile away your days, while the rest of us are busy working. That's a sweet racket you've got going, lady, but you picked the wrong mark this time."

"It's my understanding that Brett Fletcher doesn't kill himself in the line of duty. Plenty of time to philander, I think? I don't make a business of subjecting myself to possibly fatal accidents, but if I did, you would have been a wise choice. Five thousand isn't likely to break the boss of Fletcher Enterprises."

"You've done your homework well. If you had any common sense, however, you'd realize I didn't become the president of Fletcher Enterprises by being stupid."

"I didn't say you were stupid. There's a certain low animal cunning in giving me the wrong card. It might have worked, if you hadn't bragged about your new Porsche."

"Talk about cunning!" he charged, and advanced a menacing step toward her.

She shimmied aside and stood arms akimbo to continue the argument. The hostile face glaring at her grew pinker by the minute. "I didn't say intelligent, Mr. Fletcher. I said cunning—sly, but I've found you now, and by God you'll pay for what you did."

Something in the sight of this infuriating, insulting young woman robbed Brett of reason. He sensed he'd been set up, and every instinct rebelled against it. "The hell I will," he growled, and turned to leave.

She grabbed his arm. The altercation had attracted a good deal of attention by this time. Curious bathers turned to stare at the small, red-haired woman and the tall, angry man. Mila saw it and grew desperate with emotion. "If you dare to run away again, I'll call the police. I'll sue you for every penny you own," she said wildly.

Brett shook off her hand. His brows lowered, and his voice was menacing. "Don't threaten me, young lady," he said coldly. "I came here to repay any damage that was done to your car. It wasn't worth five hundred, and we both know it!"

"Five hundred!" she squealed, and grew mute with outraged shock.

"Five hundred! And I won't expect to hear you've suddenly grown lame as a result of the accident, Madam X, as you are enjoying good health today. I'm sure someone in your line of business—would prefer a cash transaction." As he spoke, he pulled out his wallet and began peeling off bills. He flung a wad of them at her feet.

She looked at the money—it seemed to be about five hundred dollars, though she didn't begin to pick it up and count. "For your information, Mr. Fletcher, my name is not Madam X. My *car* is Madam X, and it is an invaluable antique. I brought it here for the Concours d'Élégance to show and hopefully to sell. We need the money very badly."

"For a widowed mother, no doubt?" he asked, with a mocking sneer.

It was too much. His abuse of her own morals she could tolerate, but when he slighted her mother she saw red. Her hands came up, and before she knew what was happening, she had pushed him toward the edge of the pool, with every intention of pushing him in, fancy suit and all. He grabbed her arms, and a short scuffle ensued. Brett Fletcher, a distinguished and mature citizen of the town, found himself in the undignified position of publicly wrestling with a young hellcat. There was an unsuspected strength in her lithe arms and firm body. Caught off guard, he was in some peril of being pitched into the water. It was either that, or throw her in. The last thing he saw before the splash was a pair of green eyes spitting fire, and a pretty face distorted in anger.

Within two seconds, she was in the water, and he stood looking in after her, splashed from head to toe, and aghast at what he had done. He wore a blank look as he stared back at the audience that was looking at him, with a mixture of amusement and disgust.

Brett turned to leave, but some instinct of caution or chivalry caused him to hesitate, to make sure she could swim. Mila had resurfaced, spluttering and trying to rub the water from her eyes, while her hair spilled in wet strands around her shoulders. He didn't see the outraged young man in the yellow T-shirt bolting toward him. He didn't realize what was going on until Rick Healey had raised his fist and plowed a very strong punch to the corner of his jaw. Caught off balance, Mr. Fletcher went looping into the pool, missing Mila by inches.

There was a light round of applause from the on-lookers. One of them had the wits to call the man-ager. Another brought a towel for Mila, and for the next few minutes there was a general melee of confu-sion as the two dripping bodies clambered out and shook themselves off. Rick hurried to Mila's side and put a protective arm around her.

"Who the hell is that creep?" he demanded in a loud tone.

"It's Brett Fletcher," she said more softly.

"Oh my God, why didn't you tell me?"

"You didn't give me time. Let's get out of here," she said, and they hurried away to her room.

"Rick, he tried to palm me off with five hundred dollars," she said.

"Creep."

"What are you doing here anyway?"

"I have to take the Boss Mustang back. Sorry, but I have a guy coming in to see it. Oh jeez, I forgot to tell you. I phoned Hibernia Auto Restorations in New

Jersey. They have a complete machine shop, and they think they can straighten the rod that holds the headlamp, and rechrome it. They can't get it done in time for this year's show, but I thought you'd like to know."

"Good, thanks," she said distractedly.

They entered her room and Mila went into the bathroom to change into her jeans and jersey. She twisted her wet hair into a pony tail and tied it. When she came out, Rick was sitting on the bed. "I wonder if he'll sue me," he said. "Assault—maybe assault and battery. I battered him pretty good," he added, with a little smile of satisfaction.

"You were defending a woman. That's like self-defense," she assured him.

"Why were you fighting anyway? Was it over the five hundred bucks?"

"He flung it at my feet and accused me of being—I don't know what—some kind of a crook who spends her days trying to fleece rich men or something."

"What do you want to do now?" Rick asked.

"See a lawyer, I guess. Maybe you'd better write up an estimate for the damages to Madam X, so I have something in writing to show him."

"Yeah, okay. Do you want to come down to the garage with me? I mean you could drive the Boss, and save me a trip. I drove my 'Cuda here."

Mila didn't want to be alone at the hotel, where Mr. Fletcher still might be hanging around, so she agreed. She was just picking up her purse when there was a sharp rap at the door. Her heart hammered in excitement. She had a premonition who would knock so imperiously.

"You get it, Rick," she said in a breathless voice.

Chapter Three

Rick reluctantly opened the door. From across the room, Mila had a ringside seat for the proceedings. She saw that Mr. Fletcher was still wearing his wet shirt and trousers, but had removed his jacket. A swell of muscles pulled his white shirt taut across his firm chest, and beneath it a patch of black hair was visible. The wet curl hanging boyishly down the center of his forehead did nothing to alleviate the scowl that marred the rest of his face. While she took in these details, Mr. Fletcher raised his arm, and without saying a single word, delivered a crushing blow to Rick's chin that sent him reeling into the room at her feet.

Mr. Fletcher's eyes turned from Rick to Mila as he stepped in. His eyes were a navy-blue glitter of fury, and lines were carved from his nose to his lips. "Now we'll talk," he said, in an ominous voice.

Mila flew to Rick to comfort him. He sat up, rubbing his chin. "I'm okay," he mumbled, but he looked dazed.

Mila turned to Fletcher in wrath. "I hope you're satisfied," she sneered.

"I like to repay my debts."

"That's news to me!"

His lips thinned. "I don't intend to get into that argument again. You claim to have a priceless antique car. I want to see it and estimate for myself how much I owe you."

"Fine, we were just on our way to the garage to prepare an estimate for the lawyer," she said.

Her answer caused Fletcher's scowl to deepen. "I have to change. Give me the address and I'll meet you there," he said. Rick fished in his pocket and produced a dog-eared business card. "Thank you," Mr. Fletcher said, then he turned on his heel and stalked out.

"Well, you don't have to worry about his pressing charges for assault," Mila consoled her friend. "Are you all right?"

Rick moved his jaw from side to side. "I'll live," he decided. "But before we're finished with that guy, Mila, he and I are going to have a real fight. Let's go. And you'd better drive the 'Cuda. I want to give a listen to the Boss before my client test-drives it."

Mila drove to the garage in Rick's Barracuda. True to the old saying that the cobbler's child goes unshod,

Rick's own car was a mess. He was always too busy fixing other people's cars to take proper care of his own. It emitted a series of snaps and pings as she turned the key and stepped on the gas, then revved up until it sounded like a jet engine taking off. Driving in it was like driving in a very large Mexican jumping bean with four wheels. It rattled through the streets the short distance to the garage.

Mila felt strangely nervous as they waited for Mr. Fletcher to come. "I bet he'll bring a slew of lawyers," Rick said. "I have half a mind to call some of the guys in, just in case."

"What guys?"

"The guys I drag with."

Collecting a bunch of street guys didn't seem like a very good idea. Mila knew such types from her brother Bob, and while they were nice when you got to know them, the first impression was that you were dealing with punks. "Don't be silly. Even if Fletcher does bring lawyers, the meeting isn't going to degenerate into a brawl," she said.

"I wouldn't be too sure. It has both times I've met Mr. Three Piece Suit so far. You'd think a business tycoon would have more class."

"You hit him first," she reminded her knight in rumpled denim.

Brett came alone. He was thoroughly ashamed of his behavior. Why was he suddenly acting like a young hotheaded kid, instead of a serious businessman? It was that damned redhead. Something happened to him at the very sight of her. She had the uncomfortable faculty of making him lose the use of his reason. Why hadn't he recognized the name Madam X, for instance? He'd glanced at the advertisements of the Meadow Brook Concours d'Élégance. He vaguely remembered someone mentioning that a Madam X was being shown, but he had no particular interest in classic cars, and hadn't recognized that black, muddied hulk on the road last night as being one.

God, what had he gotten himself into? Repairs to a rare old antique like that could cost thousands of dollars, and he hadn't had the wits to call the police and insurance people. No wonder the woman thought he was a lunatic. But his shareholders' meeting in New York had gone well, and paying the repairs wasn't a real problem. Looming larger in his mind was that he owed Red an apology—and he still didn't even know her name. Whatever it was, he was unhappy at having to admit he was in the wrong.

It was this unpleasant duty that caused his brow to furrow when he pulled into the parking space at Rick Healey's Garage. Rick and Mila were waiting. They stood together, Rick a little to the front, as though protecting her. For some reason that he didn't care to examine, that annoyed Brett, too. He walked purposefully past Rick and addressed himself to Mila.

"Well, where is it?" he demanded curtly.

His stiff, arrogant face and the deep-blue eyes that stared at her as though she were a secondhand car caused a knot to tighten in her stomach. Mr. Fletcher had come alone, but he carried on his own well-tailored shoulders such an intimidating air of authority that she was inwardly quaking.

She had to force herself to speak bravely. "Right this way," she said, and led him into the back room. Mila was unaware of the undulation of her hips in tight jeans, and didn't notice that Mr. Fletcher was watching the show closely.

Even with the left fender crumpled and the chrome bar that held the headlights removed, Madam X was still a very impressive sight. Rick had cleaned away the traces of rain and mud, and the car glowed majestically. It was a classical beauty, the squarish body solid as a fortress. The whitewalls gleamed like new, and the chrome spokes glinted in the sunlight. The spare mounted on the front of the left side gave it a sporty air. On top of the hood a chrome eagle with raised wings poised as if ready for flight. When Brett saw the car, a glow of admiration lit his face, and a spontaneous "wow" of pleasure escaped his lips.

"So this is Madam X," he said, and went forward to run his hand lovingly over her good fender.

Mila felt gratified at his reaction, till he turned a blighting stare on her. "What on earth were you doing, driving this valuable machine at night in the rain? You must be insane."

"Not really. I just wasn't expecting to bump into you," she retaliated.

He turned and looked back at her over his shoulder. "I should have had my lawyer come with me! You've just accused yourself of causing the accident."

She was ready to snap at him, until she realized he was smiling. That smile had a curious effect on his looks. It eased the harshness she was more used to seeing. The lines between his nose and lips formed into laugh lines, and his eyes crinkled at the outer edges. There was a trace of some new sparkle in his eyes, too. Perhaps it was pleasure at catching her in the wrong, or admiration of Madam X.

"Of being bumped into by you, I should have said," she corrected hastily.

He turned back to the car, giving her time to examine him. The crease in his trousers was as sharp as a knife. His light-colored jacket looked as though it had been laminated to his broad shoulders. The back of his head showed careful barbering, a little shorter than she liked, though it suited his style. When you threw in that he was a corporate president it was easy to believe he had his choice of women.

Brett finished his examination and turned back to her. "I begin to see why my Porsche fender was ripped in two. I'm lucky I wasn't killed. They don't make them this solid these days."

"They haven't made one of these since 1933, which is why I was so upset."

"You've brought her down for the Concours, I take it?"

"That was the intention. Of course now..." She looked at the fender and frowned.

"The damage doesn't look that serious. Couldn't you get a new fender put on in two days?"

Rick, who had come up behind them, rolled his eyes ceiling-ward. "Jeez, you don't just slap any old fender on a car like this. Cadillac hasn't made parts for these old cars in decades."

"Obviously," Brett said, "but I'm sure it would be possible to buy a reproduction. Why, you can buy reproductions of all kinds of whole cars," he informed them.

"Reproductions!" Rick and Mila shouted in unison, followed by a loud denunciation.

"Why not just patch it up with bondo!" Rick jeered.

"Did I say a dirty word?" Brett asked in confusion.

"Non-authentic parts mean an automatic disqualification," Rick said. "In national meets they use CCCA rules."

"Classic Car Club of America," Mila translated, when Brett continued looking confused. "Actually the Concours d'Élégance doesn't use a point system, but anyone buying the car would plan to enter it in other meets. They wouldn't be interested in a car with repro parts."

"Sort of like a thoroughbred horse show," Brett decided.

He rubbed his chin pensively, and they all began walking toward Rick's office. As Rick spent more than three-quarters of his time at the garage, his office was actually a miniature home, containing an electric kettle, hotplate, mugs and instant coffee, empty pop cans, bed, used sweaters and shirts, and more car manuals and loose pieces of paper than a library. Mila noticed Brett's eyes widen in astonishment at the mess, but he didn't say anything.

Rick began clearing the load of previously worn clothes from the chair, and Brett spoke to Mila. "From what you say, getting the car ready for this year's show is impossible."

"Yes," she said stiffly.

"Had you planned to show only, or were you hoping to sell the car?"

"I planned to sell it," she said curtly. With a memory of his sneering comment about her widowed mother, she didn't bother adding any details about the urgency of selling, or even correcting his impression that the car was hers.

"It looks as though you'll have to wait a year," he said. "I'm sorry."

"Oh, that's all right, Mr. Fletcher. We'll just have to mortgage the farm," she said, with an ironic toss of her head.

He lifted an eyebrow at her. "Or possibly even be reduced to *working* for a living," he suggested.

She ignored his gibe. "About the payment," she said.

"I still think five thousand is a bit steep for a fender, but if that's what it costs... Of course I'll want to be notified where you buy this fender, and see the bill of sale."

"Of course," she agreed. "You wouldn't want to make the mistake of trusting anyone. I'm sure that would be very bad business."

"It could be," he answered, unfazed. "Where do you hope to find this antique part?"

Rick told him about Mr. Henderson, the man in California who had a Cadillac he was using for a parts car. "There's still the lamp bar that has to be straightened out and rechromed," he added.

"Let me have a look at it," Brett said.

"You can take my word for it that it's bent," Mila said, but she took him to the back room again to see it. Rick went with them.

Brett examined it carefully. "Are you sure you're capable of handling a job like this?" he asked Rick.

Rick's jowls turned a dangerous shade of pink. "I'm a qualified Grade-A mechanic, Mr. Fletcher," he said, and pointed to the wall where some diplomas proclaimed his progress through various courses.

Brett glanced at them. "So I see, but as a mechanic, you must realize this isn't, strictly speaking, a mechanic's job."

"I know that!" Rick barked.

"Do you know someone who does this sort of work?" Brett persisted.

"Hibernia, in New Jersey. They're a good outfit."

"And Henderson in California has the other part. Where in California does Mr. Henderson live?"

"What difference does that make?" Mila asked. "You'll get the bill of sale, don't worry. I'm not planning to rip you off."

Brett turned aside as though she hadn't spoken. "Mr. Healey?" he said.

"The Henderson Restoration Center, in L.A. Mind you, I haven't been able to reach Henderson. He may not even have a fender. There's another guy in New Hampshire who's foraging for parts, too."

"Then you'd better get on the blower," Brett suggested, "or he'll beat you to it."

"Don't worry, I·will."

"It seems there's nothing more to be done today," Brett said. He reached to shake Mila's hand. She put her hand in his reluctantly. "I'm very sorry for the inconvenience, Miss... I don't know your name!" Brett said, and laughed lightly.

"Dempster. Mila Dempster," she said. He held her hand closely in his, squeezing her fingers, while he looked into her eyes. There was some discomfort in the atmosphere, though she sensed that Brett was trying to patch up the misunderstanding, and do the right thing.

"Mila Dempster. I'll remember that."

"Don't worry, I'll keep in touch," she answered tartly and withdrew her fingers.

"Is that a threat—or a promise, Mila?"

The tension was still there, but it had taken on a new tinge. What was he thinking that lent that sparkle to his eyes? Whatever it was, it made her feel suddenly warm around the neck.

"A threat, Mr. Fletcher," she said.

He threw back his head and laughed, his white teeth showing straight and regular. "I can live with a threat like that," he said. "Can I drop you somewhere, since I've put your car out of commission? Or do you use

Madam X for tooling around town?" he asked with a bold smile.

"Of course not. I'm staying here a while with Rick. Thanks anyway, Mr. Fletcher."

"The name's Brett, with two t's." He gave a long, slow smile, as though to impress the name on her, not that she was in any danger of forgetting it. She watched, feeling like a snake in the hands of an Indian fakir. Something in him held her motionless, speechless, as they went on looking.

At last he turned to Rick. "I expect to be hearing from you very soon, Mr. Healey. Sorry about . . ." He hunched his shoulders and smiled.

Mila noticed that Rick was not so hypnotized as she had been by that smile. She already suspected her reaction was sex-related.

"That's okay. I guess you owed me one."

"Now we're square. And by the way, you have a formidable right."

"Thanks. Your left isn't bad, either." Then Rick smiled a small smile, as if he didn't really want to, and came forward to shake hands.

"Friends?" Brett asked.

"Now that you've punched me out, too, I guess we are."

"There's a moral in there somewhere." Brett smiled. "I never make an enemy when I can make a friend."

"You must be thinking of going into politics," Mila said casually.

"Not really—I'd prefer to *keep* my friends. Good-bye."

Brett let himself out of the office, and soon the sound of his car starting up was heard. "What did you think of Mr. Three Piece Suit?" Rick asked, with a disparaging smile.

"I guess he's all right."

"He was trying to pick you up, doll face. Why didn't you go with him?"

"I don't care much for pickups," she said. "Why don't you phone Henderson now, Rick?"

Rick made the call, but Mr. Henderson was still not in. Mila decided to go back to the hotel and take that swim she'd been looking forward to.

"Will you be here tomorrow?" Rick called as she walked toward the door.

"Yes . . . no. I don't know. I haven't decided."

"I can arrange about the parts and call you at home. Not much point sticking around. That hotel's going to cost you a bundle."

"Yeah. I'll...I'll let you know if I decide to go home tonight."

There were only about seven thousand people in the city of Rochester during the summer when the university students had all gone home. It was virtually surrounded by the larger areas of Rochester Hills and Oakland Township, but it was a small, self-contained area, easy to get around in. In such a small town it was a short walk to her hotel, but once she'd had her swim, there wouldn't be much to do. Going home was a temptation, yet for some reason, Mila wasn't in a hurry to leave. In fact, she felt a pronounced inclination to stay.

She changed back into her green suit and finally had the swim. Her suit was still wet, which made it clammy and unpleasant to get into, but once she was in the water, she felt better. She did forty laps, to work off the tensions of the day. Then she sat in a lounge chair and tried to relax, to ease that knot of—what?—that was still coiled like a spring inside her. She could no longer blame it on worry or the fear that Brett was trying to escape paying. She'd confessed the whole thing to her mother, so that wasn't it. Where was the ease that should have come with having the problem solved, even if not quite to her satisfaction?

As soon as she closed her eyes, a vision of Brett Fletcher popped into her head, so clearly she could almost think he was there, smiling at her from those enigmatic dark eyes. In her mind's eye, he wore that assessing smile she had caught him at when he was watching her the first time at the pool. Rick thought he was trying to pick her up. Maybe he'd phone the hotel. Was that the reason she wasn't in a hurry to go home? Brett Fletcher, the playboy—what did she want with someone like him? She usually went out with school teachers or accountants, staid and reliable businessmen. What did any woman want with a man like Brett? some little voice asked her. He was gorgeous.

The sun was warm, caressing her face, her arms and legs with a sensuous heat that seemed to penetrate to her vitals, melting her bones and organs, till she felt like a puddle of soft butter. Oh, it felt so good, so relaxing. But the knot was still coiled inside her.

She bet Brett's hands, with those long, shapely fingers, would feel good on her flesh, too. She could almost imagine she was feeling them stroking her cheek, but it was only her hair. She brushed it, pretending it was Brett's fingers.

"A call for you, Miss Dempster," a voice said at her shoulder.

She jumped six inches from her chair. "What?"

"A phone call, Miss Dempster. You were expecting one earlier, I believe?" The bellboy handed her the phone, with an impish smile that told her he had heard of the episode at the pool.

"Thank you," she said coolly, and took it from him.

"Hello."

"Hello, Mila. It's Brett. Don't hang up, please."

A little frisson scurried up her spine at the cashmere softness of his voice, richly smooth. She leaned back and smiled. "I have no intention of hanging up, Brett. What can I do for you?"

"Are you going to be in town this evening?"

"Yes, I am," she said, with no hesitation.

"Have you made your plans yet?"

"I was planning an early night. Why?" She was glad he couldn't see the flush that she knew was on her cheeks or the light of hope in her eyes.

"Will you have dinner with me? An early dinner," he added.

"I have to eat. What did you have in mind?" Her brain was already scurrying over her wardrobe, regretting she hadn't brought more clothes. She only had a two-year-old cotton dress that she'd brought along in case she and Rick might take in a movie.

"I thought we might drive down to Pontiac. There's a nice seafood place there. Do you like lobster?"

"I adore lobster."

"Seven early enough for you?"

"Seven's fine."

"Good. I had a bit of trouble getting hold of you. Are you at the pool—again?"

"Yes."

"One dunking a day not enough for you?" He laughed.

She felt a rankle of discontent at that laugh. She still owed him one. "It's not nice to gloat, Brett," she chided.

"From the sound of that purr, it's not safe to gloat, either. I am really very sorry we got off to such a poor start. Shall we start over again, pretend it never happened?"

"We can try," she agreed.

"Fair enough. I'll pick you up at seven. I have to go now. Bye."

"Goodbye."

"I'll pick you up." The phrase displeased her. That was what Rick said Brett had been trying to do. And now he'd succeeded. She had a feeling Brett Fletcher usually succeeded in his endeavors. She shouldn't have accepted. Someone should thwart Brett Fletcher, just once. Depending on what he had in mind, he might just find his plans upset before the night was over.

The speed with which she hopped up and went to her room to prepare for the date didn't suggest thwarting, but Mila didn't think of that. She was too busy worrying whether her blue cotton dress was good enough for a fancy seafood restaurant. To be perfectly truthful, it wasn't the lobster's opinion she was worried about, or the other guests', either. It was Brett Fletcher's.

Chapter Four

As she stood in front of the mirror, Mila knew she looked all wrong. The attempt to appear sophisticated by drawing her hair up didn't match the simple blue cotton dress. She liked the dress, with its scooped neck, small sleeves and full skirt, but it just wasn't right for going out with a sophisticated man like Brett Fletcher. She pulled the pins from her hair and fluffed her curls out with the brush. At least everything matched now—she looked like a nice small-town person. Well, that's what she was, wasn't it? She couldn't change her whole persona for one date.

Rather than coming to her room, Brett called her from the front desk and she went down. He was wearing a light summer suit. He seemed to know the hotel manager, to judge by the familiar way they stood talking and laughing. Still at a distance, she had a chance to look at her date. Tall, handsome and debonair, he was the kind of man she secretly admired, but had little chance to go out with in Muskegon. Then he looked over and saw her, and across the lobby she felt the magnetic pull of him. Without knowing she did it, she smiled and hastened her steps. Brett introduced her to Jack Orr, the proprietor and manager of the hotel.

"So this is the young lady who made you forget to pick up your money," Jack said, smiling at her. "You had Brett in such a state he stomped out of the pool and left a wad of money on the floor this afternoon." She was surprised to hear Brett had been that deeply affected.

"A regrettable incident." Brett smiled, and peeled off a bill. "There's a finder's fee for the honest bellboy who turned it in. We want to encourage that sort of thing. Good night, Jack."

With a wave to the manager, they were off. "You realize, of course, that you've done considerable harm to my staid reputation," he told her. "It ill becomes a corporation president to throw a woman in the pool."

"We were going to forget all that, remember?"

"Indeed I do. You'll notice I didn't drive my poor injured Porsche. I didn't want any reminders of past indiscretions, and here we can't seem to talk about anything else but our various . . . accidents. It was an accident, you know, that dunking. Self-defense is what it was."

"Is it my turn to apologize? I don't usually attack strangers, either. Sorry."

He opened the door of a white station wagon bearing the name Fletcher Enterprises on the side, and she got in. "I've taken my Porsche in for a new fender," he explained. "I wanted this chance to make up for the past. And now we'll really forget it."

He turned the key and they were off. The conversation from then on was as if they had never met before. "Where are you from, Mila?" he asked.

"Muskegon. It's a small town on the west side of the state, just bordering Lake Michigan."

"You're just here for the car show, I take it?"

"Yes."

"Since Madam X is so valuable, why don't you take her to Pebble Beach? That's the most famous show in the country, I believe?"

"The most famous, and the most distant. It's very expensive to have a car hauled all the way to California. I won't say a word about how dangerous it would be to drive it."

"Still, it seems like an investment that might pay off in the long run."

"I was in a bit of a hurry. How far is Pontiac?" she asked, to change the subject.

"Just ten miles or so, through some of the prettiest countryside in the state."

As they left the city and drove through the hilly countryside, along twisting roads dotted with orchards and farms, Mila admired the idyllic view. Autumn had not yet begun to turn the leaves to red and orange, but the setting sun bathed them in shining gold. After a moment's silence, she said in a stilted voice, "What does Fletcher Enterprises do?"

He explained about his factories that did various kinds of metal work. "This is car country hereabouts," he said. "Close to Detroit, though you'd never guess it in this peaceful setting. I make a lot of components for cars."

"Are you an engineer?"

"I was, but I'm more involved in the business end of it now. The reason I was in such a hurry to 'leave the scene of the crime' is that I had an important meeting in New York, and had to catch the plane last night. If I'd missed it, I'd have had to get up at five in the morning and arrive half asleep. In the confusion, I accidentally gave you the wrong card."

Before long they were on the outskirts of Pontiac, and Brett drove in at a place whimsically called The Lobster-Shack. "Some shack," Mila said, as she peered at the place through the lengthening shadows of twilight. It looked like a private mansion that had been turned into a restaurant. It was in the English Tudor style, half-timbered with brick portions and leaded windows. "I'll probably be the only woman here in a cotton dress."

He regarded her with a slow smile that had the curious effect of making her melt. "I don't know whether you'll be the only one, but I can guarantee you'll be the most beautiful."

"I—I only brought one dress with me. I thought Rick and I might go to a movie or something," she babbled.

"Is it more than business with you and Healey?"

"Rick's in love," she said, and looked at him. Was she imagining that swift shadow that passed over his face—was it the effect of the shifting shadows? "With Madam X," she added.

She certainly didn't imagine that he opened his lips in a smile, and that his eyes were glowing warmly. "He has good taste," Brett said, then turned and opened his door. When he came to her door to open it he added, "I prefer younger ladies myself." He took her elbow and they walked to the carved oaken door of the restaurant.

Again Brett was apparently a friend of the manager, for he was made welcome by name. "I reserved your favorite table, by the window," the man said. "The ducks and geese haven't bedded down yet. If you hurry, you'll be able to say good-night to Esmeralda."

From their table, they had a view of a duckpond, where half a dozen waterfowl waddled awkwardly around the edge, and a few ducks paddled more gracefully in the water.

"Which one's Esmeralda?" Mila asked.

"She's the big white lady, the mother of the brood." He tapped on the window, trying to attract her attention, but Esmeralda turned her tail to him and waddled off.

"She's playing hard to get. She knows I have no taste for easy conquests," he said. "A cocktail before dinner, or would you prefer wine?"

"What's good here?"

"Everything," he said compehensively. "They make a great Bloody Caesar."

"Is that the one with clam juice?"

"That's it."

"Thanks for the warning. I'll have wine."

"We'll order a bottle, and I'll join you later. I need my vitamins first."

There was a lapse in the conversation, and to fill it, Brett asked, "How come you put Madam X in the hands of a young fellow like Healey? I thought you'd want an expert for the job."

"Oh, Rick is an expert," she said, latching on to this conversational gambit eagerly. "He's been working with cars ever since he could walk. He and Madam X go back a long way."

"From what I've seen of his own wheels around town, I thought he was a hot rod freak. He drives an old crate covered in rust."

"Not rust, Brett. Primer. His 383 Magnum 'Cuda is a rare car, in the process of being fixed up for drag racing."

"I repeat, why are you letting him get his hands on Madam X?"

"Well, it's kind of hard to explain. He's a super mechanic. His job is ordinary repairs to cars—engines, I mean, not body work, and he does it very well indeed. His hobby is drag racing, so he knows all about muscle cars, and souping up engines and things. Then the cultural aspect of his life is restoring antiques. He helped Dad fix up Madam X, and since he's right in Rochester, naturally I took her to him to be prepped for the show. He'll do a good job. You couldn't do better than send your car to Rick.''

"My car's still under dealership warranty."

"I didn't mean your Porsche. The station wagon you drove tonight, though—if you ever need a good mechanic for it, I'd recommend Rick highly. His whole life is cars, that's the thing. Anything to do with cars. He's kind of an automotive general practitioner."

She felt this topic had been stretched to its limits, and was relieved when the drinks arrived. She was surprised to see Brett remove the stick of celery, since he had mentioned needing his vitamins. "Aren't you going to eat it? It looks so nice—the heart," she pointed out.

He passed her the plate, and as she was hungry, she took the celery and began chewing it. She rather regretted it when the crisp celery made its unique racket as she chewed it. She ate more slowly, but still the crunch continued. She looked up through her lashes in embarrassment, and saw Brett smiling at her. "Now you know why I let on I didn't want it," he said, and took the stalk from her to chew unabashedly. "I didn't want you to take me for a rube. Actually, true sophistication is above such foolishness—if you happen to have a taste for celery."

"I don't try to pass myself off as a sophisticate," she said simply.

"I know. That's what's so attractive about you. Sophistication actually has bad overtones—a lack of genuineness, naturalness."

She looked surprised at this unexpected compliment. Sophistication had always seemed a highly prized thing to Mila. "Muskegon's a pretty small town. You don't have much chance to become sophisticated there," she said.

"Your naïveté's worn a bit thin though," he teased. "You were quick to jump to the conclusion I was trying to squeak out of paying for your car repairs. Such sophistication never occurred to me. I'm a small-town lad myself. I was born and grew up here in Rochester. A charming place. We have all kinds of cultural facilities—universities, festivals, theatre, even a symphony. Of course I'm talking about Greater Rochester now—all within a stone's throw of home. I never had any hankering to move to a city. My work takes me around, but I consider myself very much a small-town guy." She didn't think many men from Rochester drove Porsche cars and wore such expensive suits, but she nodded as if understanding.

"What do you do in Muskegon?" he asked. "Do you work?"

"Of course! Did you think I was a millionaire?"

"Not necessarily, but working women aren't usually at leisure during the week. And they don't own cars worth a fortune, either," he mentioned, with a curious glance.

"The car's a family heirloom. I teach school, grade five. It's considered the most interesting grade in public school. The kids are old enough to have settled down, and not old enough yet to become behavioral problems. A fierce glare is usually all it takes to control them," she said.

"Now I understand where you perfected your wicked stare. I knew it made me feel like a schoolboy. But you don't look much like the teachers I had when I was a kid."

"I'm plenty strict! You have to be," she said, and before she knew it, she was being led to revelations about her work.

The waiter came and tied big white bibs around their necks, making her feel more like a student than a teacher. She had to smile, to see the elegant Brett Fletcher wearing a bib.

"Shall we two sophisticates manqué get right down to pulling the legs off these critters and stuffing ourselves?" he asked.

As she dunked the succulent pink pieces of meat into the clarified butter, and sipped wine, Mila found herself perfectly at ease with this man who used to intimidate her. Before the meal was over, she was so at home with him she even pointed out that he'd left a joint of claw full of meat, and when he said it was too much trouble to get it out, she cracked it apart for him and wielded the small fork to extract the meat in a neat piece.

All the time they talked easily, as though they'd been friends for years. Brett told her how he had started his business, making ball bearings for wheels in a little wooden hut with second-hand equipment and a staff of five. "At the end of the second month I had to sell my car to pay the workers. I was about to declare myself bankrupt when I got my first big contract. *Then* the bank lent me enough money to build my first real factory. That's the way they work. They're always willing to lend money to anyone who doesn't need it."

"But you did need it."

"Ah, that's the way I work, always suspecting the other fellow. But I don't have to tell you that, do I, Mila?" he teased. "I never looked back. There's a great satisfaction in being in business for yourself."

"Maybe I should rent a hundred kids and open my own school," she laughed.

"Like the man with the contract to keep the bronze statue in the park polished. He saved for five years and bought a statue to go into business for himself. Not very profitable, but of course a woman always has the option of producing her own children."

"Also not very profitable." She nodded unthinkingly.

"Next year you'll be rich, after you sell Madam X." She considered telling him the truth about the car, that it wasn't hers, but she was having a good time and wanted to keep that subject silent. "You're not interested in having a family?" he asked.

"Some day, perhaps. For the present, I like my life."

"I suppose you travel in summers—Europe, Greece, etcetera?"

"Europe?" she asked, blinking. "Good heavens, no. I've never been there. I'd love to go."

"Why didn't you? Why did you buy that car? It must have cost a small fortune."

"It's not mine," she admitted. Then, as he persisted, she said, "It's my mother's life insurance policy."

"Is your father... I notice you haven't mentioned him."

"Yes, he passed away of cancer a year ago," she said, and looked at the table. Candlelight produced little flames in the depth of her wineglass. It looked so strange, to see fire in a liquid. They'd made a shambles of the nice white tablecloth, with bits of lobster shell and butter splattered around their plates. She stared hard at these things, to keep the image of her father from coming to her. Concentration pulled her lips down at the corners. The candlelight caused a long, curved shadow of her lashes to form on her cheeks, and tinted her hair to gold. She could no longer keep the cherished image at bay. It loomed up in her mind's eye, but she blinked back the hot tears. It must be the wine that was making her sentimental. She hadn't cried over Dad for weeks now. Why did the tears have to come on this special night?

She saw Brett's slender hands reaching across the table, taking her fingers in his. They felt warm and strong and protective. "I'm sorry. I shouldn't have asked," he said softly.

"It's all right," she said gruffly, and pulled her hands away. "It's just that sometimes I remember him so vividly. And it's hard on Mom, being alone. Without him, I mean. They did everything together. We used to go for picnics in Madam X," she said, and suddenly Brett was filling her glass again, and she was telling him how proud her father had been of Madam X.

"She was practically a member of the family."

"It's odd Cadillac gave her such an imaginative name. That's rather unusual."

"It's unique, like the car. The name came from a melodrama, but they dropped the *e* from Madame. It was a popular stage play in the twenties. The car's inventor—Harley Earl—saw the play and liked it so well he stole the name. *Madame X* was also made into a movie a couple of times."

Brett gazed at her, encouraging her to talk by adding a question from time to time. "I believe I caught it on the late show with Lana Turner. A noble lady who sacrificed everything for love."

"That's it. Dad's all-time favorite movie, of course. But the car really is unique."

"The windshield tilts at a peculiar angle."

"Yes, it's raked at eighteen degrees to give the sedan the sporty look of a convertible."

"I'm surprised your mother would think of selling the car, as Madam X seems to be a bona fide member of the family."

"Oh, Mom hates her. They've been rivals for years. Many's the time we had to keep linens and drapes and clothes till they were worn out, so Madam X could have some expensive repair. As I said, she's our insurance policy. The medical bills ate up Dad's savings."

Brett sat still, not rigid but still, listening attentively. "Is money a problem at home? An urgent problem, I mean? Your mother's not in danger of losing the house, or anything like that?"

"No, of course not," she said, but so hastily and with so little conviction that he suspected she was lying to save his feelings.

"Damn," he said softly. Her head jerked up in surprise.

"I'm a thoughtless jerk. I was just remembering my crack about your widowed mother. I had no idea, Mila. Why didn't you tell me?"

"It's all right. We'll sell next year. The price will only go up."

"This is my fault. *I'll* buy Madam X."

"No! Don't be silly. We expect to get about a quarter of a million for her. You said you're expanding—that welding factory—you can't afford her."

"I can always get a loan. It'd be an investment."

She shook her head firmly. "No, antique cars need the kind of care that only an aficionado can give. They should be owned by someone like Dad, who's willing to pamper them to death. They're a lot of trouble, Brett. Thanks for the offer, but it's all right—really."

"If you run into problems, come to me. Remember what I said, banks only lend you money when you don't need it. You don't want to have to mortgage Madam X. This is my fault, and if anyone's inconvenienced, it should be me. I can always lend you a couple of thousand in a pinch. Will you promise me?"

She looked him in the eye. The arrogance and the anger were gone. She saw only concern, or perhaps it was pity. She didn't want pity. "No," she said bluntly. "We have family, aunts and uncles who'd be glad to help in a crisis. You don't borrow money from relative strangers. Thanks anyway for the offer. It was kind of you. You just pay for Madam's repairs, and we'll be square."

He wasn't offended at her bluntness. He nodded his head in approval. "All right. But the offer still stands, just in case."

The waiter came with the dessert menu, and as he removed their bibs, they put the bothersome talk of money behind them. "I'm feeling extremely gluttonous," Mila admitted. "I'm going to try the strawberry shortcake."

"A wise choice, but mine is wiser. I'm having Paul's pecan pie."

"Oh, that sounds good!" Mila exclaimed, undecided.

"The crust melts in your mouth, and the syrup—ah, irresistible. So sweet it curls your ears. I'll have to jog four miles tomorrow to atone for it."

"But I love strawberries."

"The lady will have strawberry shortcake and a small piece of pecan pie," Brett said, "and I'll have just the pecan pie."

"Not both!" she said, but the waiter had already left.

"If you can't eat it, take it home in a doggie bag," Brett suggested. "You've got to try Paul's pecan pie. It's a legend in its own time."

"Actually, that's inaccurate. A legend is a story that's come down from the past," she said almost automatically, as she had corrected the same error several times in school.

"Or a popular myth of more recent origin, I think," he objected.

"That's how words lose their true meaning. You are abetting the corruption of the English language, Brett."

"If you say so, teacher, but wait till you taste the pecan pie. It's worth it."

It was divinely rich, but after the shortcake, she could only manage one forkful. They sat over their coffee, looking out the window, where night had fallen, and only the moonbeams were playing on the pond. A comfortable mood surrounded them.

"It's too bad they don't have a dance floor here," Brett said. "Would you like to go dancing?"

"I don't think the lobster and shortcake would. They seem pretty content just as they are. That was a gourmet feast, Brett. Four star."

"A legend in its own time?" he asked, smiling.

She filled their cups again and sat back, sated with food and wine. The crowd in the dining room was thinning. It was an elegant assembly that she enjoyed looking at. A couple across the room rose and suddenly spotted Brett. They came to his table before leaving. Mila looked with interest at the woman. She was about thirty and extremely elegant. Her blond hair was the color of moonlight, cascading over the shoulders of a chic black dress, but more noticeable was the predatory gleam in her eye, and the way she was staring at them. She made Mila feel guilty. Who could she be?

Chapter Five

The blond woman glided forward. "Brett, I didn't see you, hiding behind the palms. I wish I'd known you were here. I might have guessed—your favorite restaurant. I see you've been stuffing yourself with pecan pie, as usual," she chided. "We could have had dinner together. Harvey has been boring me to distraction with technical talk that he knows I don't understand."

Her partner, Harvey, said hello, and Brett made introductions. The woman's name was Bonnie Clarke, and as the man's name was Clarke, too, Mila assumed they were husband and wife. She noticed that Bonnie's manner was flirtatious, but as it was quite open, it seemed that Bonnie was just one of those women who played up to all men, regardless. Harvey worked for Brett as manager of one of the factories, to judge by the few words he said about some shipment.

"Oh, this brother of mine," Bonnie said. Mila took a closer look at them, and noticed the family resemblance in coloring and build. Both of them were tall and blond. "All he ever talks about is business. Let's talk about something more interesting." She looked at the two empty chairs at the table for four, but didn't sit down, nor did Brett invite them to.

"Let's talk about going home," Harvey suggested.

"It's early," Bonnie said. "I'm stopping off at the club for a drink on the way. The Hampton Golf Club, I mean," she added, and looked to see that the name had registered with Brett. "I'll be there for an hour or so, if you and Mila feel thirsty, Brett. There'll be people dancing—just to records, unfortunately."

"Tomorrow's a working day," Brett said, glancing at his watch.

"You're the boss. You can go in any time you like, lucky man." Bonnie smiled admiringly. In fact, admiration was the best way to describe her whole manner. And though Bonnie half-heartedly included Mila in the invitation to the club, the invitation in her eyes was directed only to Brett.

"We'll see," Brett said.

"I suppose that means no," Bonnie said, pouting attractively. "In any case, I'll see you tomorrow night at eight."

"I haven't forgotten your party. I'll be there," Brett said. Mila thought his manner toward the intruders was becoming a little brusque. She noticed, too, that he'd spoken rather quickly to remove the idea that he had a private date with Bonnie.

"Feel free to bring your little friend, if she'll still be in town," Bonnie said. Her eyes were assessing Mila in the way that any woman with blood in her veins recognized as sizing up the competition. No matter how friendly her manner was, Bonnie's eyes were as green as grass. "Are you just passing through, Mila? You must watch out for Brett. He has a built-in antenna for finding any new woman in town within twelve hours." She turned to smile jokingly at Brett. "Or do you just haunt the hotel, pouncing on any pretty woman who stops, Brett?"

Mila heard that "little friend" and the hint that she was a pickup with a stab of annoyance. Of course Brett didn't literally haunt the hotel lobbies trying to pick up women—Bonnie was just taking a swipe at him because he was with a date.

"I've known Brett longer than one day actually," Mila said coolly. "I'll be checking out tomorrow, so I'll have to pass on your party. Thanks, anyway."

"Pity. Eight o'clock tomorrow evening, Brett. Don't be late. We're counting on you to send over those extra glasses you promised from the company cafeteria."

"Good night, Bonnie, Harvey," Brett said, and the couple left. "Harvey's the manager of my machine shop," he explained to Mila. It was hard to read from his expression whether he was embarrassed, or slightly annoyed at the interruption. Either reaction seemed out of place, unless there was some reason he didn't want Bonnie to see him with another woman. Only one reason occurred to her.

"Does Bonnie work for you, too?"

"No, she's an artist, a very good one. She runs a local gallery, and is busy on the Rochester Arts Commission. I bought the machine shop from their father. Harvey knew a lot about it and needed a job, so he runs it for me. They're a nice family—good friends."

"So I gathered," she said, with a noncommittal nod. "As you said, it's getting late and you have work tomorrow. Shall we go now? Dinner was marvelous. Thank you."

"My pleasure. Next time you're in town, send out a bleep and I'll trace you on my antenna. You are definitely leaving tomorrow, aren't you?"

"I have no reason to stay. And even cheap hotels cost money."

He drew out his wallet and counted bills to leave on the table. "Jack Orr won't appreciate your calling his hotel cheap."

"Relatively speaking. I should have said modest."

He put his hand on her elbow as they walked out to the station wagon. "Many things are relative, and subject to revision under varying circumstances. If I could provide free accommodations and a reason to stay over, would you consider it—revise your decision?"

"If you're going to offer to pay my hotel bill some-where, please don't. It would be a shame to spoil a lovely evening," she said stiffly.

He held her door, and as she got in, she noticed a look of surprise on his face. That wasn't what he meant, then, and she was glad.

Once the station wagon was moving through the dark night, she could no longer see him clearly. She sat rather uncomfortably, wondering how to continue the conversation without falling into some double-entendre type of talk.

"You're strangely uncurious," Brett said, slanting a glance at her. "You didn't ask me what the reason was."

"I'm listening."

"Bonnie invited you to her party. The Clarkes have very good parties."

Seeing Bonnie again held very little attraction. Seeing Brett again, though—she was minutely aware of the attraction in him. She looked at his profile, sharp and clear and strong, and peculiarly intimate in the shadowed confines of the car. He wouldn't be in-viting her to Bonnie's party if he were involved with Bonnie... "She was only being polite. I wouldn't know anyone there," she parried.

"You'd know the hostess, and you'd know Har-vey, and me."

"Thanks, but I don't think so. I don't have a suit-able dress with me."

"Rochester is small, but not that small. You could find something. I know I'm being rudely persistent, but the thing is, I *have* to go to that party. Bonnie's annual do is a big deal in Rochester. I accepted the invitation ages ago, and since Harvey is one of my managers . . .''

She could tell him one of two truths to quell his insistence, and debated silently for a moment whether to say she just plain didn't want to go, or she really shouldn't spend the money on a dress. "It would mean staying another night at the hotel, as well as buying a new dress. I'm sure it'll be a great party, but since most of the people will be strangers to me, you can understand why I'm refusing."

"Pardon me while I go on being rude as hell," he said, with a charming smile that robbed the words of anything but flattery. "Muskegon is nearly one hundred fifty miles away, and I assume you'll be coming back for the Concours. Wouldn't it be easier to stay over? I mentioned free accommodation, and being a very proper teacher of children, you immediately flew to the conclusion that I intended to put you up at a hotel and ruin your reputation. That wasn't what I had in mind."

"Actually, I'm not at all sure I'll come back for the show. I was only going because Madam X was entered."

"Oh." He sat silent a minute, but she knew from the way he was worrying his lip that he still hadn't given up.

Curious, she asked, "What accommodation did you have in mind, if not paying my hotel bill?"

"I have a company guesthouse that's empty at the moment. It's really a side wing of my own house, but with a separate entrance and facilities. You can lock the adjoining door, but please don't throw away the key, or you'll starve to death. My cook serves the meals in the guest wing, and she cooks them in my kitchen. There's nothing in the arrangement to jeopardize the reputation of an upstanding teacher. Or even a sitting down one," he added lightly, as he peered at her through the shadows.

She was gratified at his eagerness and curious to see his house, but the idea of attending Bonnie's party as an outsider was still far from tempting. "I don't know," she said uncertainly.

"Ah, you're a brave woman, to think of leaving that class-A mechanic alone to have his way with your Madam X. I'd sit on his tail until she's repaired if I were you," he said, trying a new tack.

"For a whole year?" she said, laughing.

"For a week at least."

They drove past Rick's garage. The lights were on, but Mila knew from the leather jackets she could see through the window that Rick wasn't working. He was talking about drag cars with his racing friends.

"You're really quite shameless, Brett," she said, shaking her head.

"Nonsense, I'm thoroughly ashamed of myself. I'll give myself a stern talking-to when I get home. But meanwhile..."

"Meanwhile, that's my hotel up ahead."

"So it is. Where did it come from?" he asked, feigning surprise that the building was there, even though it was where it had been for fifty years. "If I were with some woman I was eager to be rid of, do you think it would be there, so convenient? I bet it would have moved to San Francisco."

"You're seriously weird, Brett. Hey, you passed the hotel!"

"I'm still working on you. I'm going to drive you past the Fletcher Arms Hotel. That's the name of my guest suite. I just christened it this minute. I rather like it. Gives the place a touch of class, don't you think?"

"Elegant."

"It has tennis courts. No one to play with during the day, of course, but think of the exercise you'll get, hitting the ball then jumping the net to hit it back to yourself. There's a nice pool to push people into, too."

"I'm surprised you have so much trouble getting clients, with all those amenities. And it's free, too, you say."

"*Mi casa, su casa.* This is it right up ahead," he said pointing out the window.

She looked and had to concentrate on suppressing a gasp of surprise. Floodlights illuminated the house, which was square and three stories high, with massive chimneys. The beautiful, very large, old brick house, looked like one of the stately homes of England in its parklike setting, with an expanse of manicured lawn, edged with hedges and flower beds.

"The guest house is just around the edge of the drive," he said.

"It's . . . lovely," she said, and felt the word inadequate.

"It's ridiculous, really, one man living in a place that size, which is why I turned the west wing into a guesthouse."

"Why did you buy it?"

"I liked it," he said simply. "There are half a dozen of these big old houses along this stretch of road. The Clarkes live just a quarter of a mile farther on. There was a big brouhaha about turning this house into some kind of a commercial venture when the original owner died. The local historical society got upset about it. Bonnie came to me for help. Actually, it was her idea that I buy it, and I'm glad I did."

"I see" was all Mila said, but she had a sinking feeling that Bonnie and Brett were more than good friends after all. Why did she suggest what house he should buy, and why did he buy it, when he obviously didn't need such a big place for just himself?

"Would you like to go in and check out the rooms?" he asked.

"I don't think so. I'd really like to go home—back to the hotel, I mean."

He nodded his agreement and turned the car around. There was no more insisting after that, nor was there any more nonsensical talk. Brett certainly wasn't sulking, but he accepted her answer, and returned to his normal manner. He drove the car into the parking lot of the hotel, around the corner from the front entrance, and turned off the ignition.

"Thank you for a very nice evening, Mila," he said simply.

"Thank you—once again."

"I hope we can do this again some time—soon, I mean."

She was rather sad to realize how unlikely this was. Oh, she might see him once more, when she came to pick up Madam X after the work was done on her. But that would be months from now, and there wasn't enough in between to survive such a long absence.

"I'll call you if I'm ever in town again—I mean *when* I'm in town."

He took her hand and held it. She thought he was experiencing some of the sensations she felt. His lips were twisted into a sad little smile, and when he spoke, there was no joy in his voice. "You won't, you know. Once you've been home for a few days, you'll forget about tonight, and start remembering less pleasant meetings, when you ended up wet, from rain or pool water. You'll remember my punching Rick out. I don't even know why I did it."

"Because he hit you first, and you always pay your debts," she reminded him.

"Was that my excuse?" he asked, surprised.

"I thought it was a little limp myself."

"It was a lie," he said. "This is why I did it." Then he pulled her into his arms and kissed her.

A gentle good-night kiss seemed appropriate. She put her arms around his neck and returned the light pressure of his lips. That was all it took. At the first sign of acquiescence his arms tightened, crushing her against his solid chest until she was gasping for air. His lips firmed and instead of becoming alarmed, Mila felt a heady surge of excitement. She moved her hands through the rough texture of his hair, along his neck, revelling in the sudden and unexpected intimacy. A quiver shot through her when she felt his tongue nudge her lips open. The absorbing touch of his tongue stroking hers heightened her perceptions.

She was aware of the musky scent that emanated faintly from him, a mere suggestion of woodlands. She felt the blunt ends of his hair against her fingers, felt her breasts molding to the contours of his chest, felt his chest rise and fall with his breaths. Suddenly one of his hands rose to brush over her hair, pulling it back from her neck, and his lips left hers to nuzzle the smoothness of her throat. The scooped-neckline of her dress fell away, allowing him to press lower, until his lips were caressing the top of her breasts with entrancing familiarity. When she felt his moist tongue glide across her skin, she sensed danger. She cupped his jaw in her hand and lifted his face slowly, so she could see him. His eyes were a diamond glitter of desire in the darkness, and his breath fanning her cheek was becoming ragged.

"This is a really lousy excuse for punching Rick out," she said, but somehow it came out in a provocative croon.

"The best reason in the world, Mila," he murmured, and turned his head to nip her fingers.

"What reason?"

His lips moved to hers, gently stroking, teasing, taunting. They slid up her cheek to her earlobe. He took one in his mouth and bit gently. "Jealousy—and I didn't even know it. I thought I just hated the poor guy. It was you, all the time." His words were soft as a sigh, gentle as a zephyr, and warm as the sun.

How could such soft sayings have such violent results? They burned like a flame in her head, seared a trail through her body, leaving her weak. Jealous! Brett was jealous. Her voice when she answered was breathless. "Silly. Rick doesn't mean anything to me."

"Kiss me," he ordered impatiently, and claimed her lips again for a ruthless kiss. His tongue immediately claimed her mouth. Its marauding motions were more demanding than before, circling the perimeters and claiming it for his own. As he kissed her deeply, his fingers found her breasts and squeezed lightly with kneading motions until she could feel the tips of her nipples firm with passion. She should make him stop—but she wanted it to go on. Some wildness was loose in her, some insatiable desire. She wanted—oh, she wanted *him*, all of him.

When his fingers brushed inside her bra, she felt the hair on her arms rise in appreciation, and a lethargy invaded her being. Her bones had turned to putty, without resistance or a will of their own. She held her breath in wonder while the stroking of his warm fingers continued, seeking out the tips of her breasts. And all the time his lips held her captive in a fiercely sweet kiss that was robbing her of reason. What must he think of her—and on the first date, too?

She tried to ease away, but his hands cupped her shoulder and held her close to him, where she wanted to be. But when one hand began to move to her breast again, she firmed her decision. She pulled away forcefully and said, "I really have to go now, Brett."

"Come home with me," he urged.

Not "come home and stay in the guest suite" but "come home with me." He thought that because she'd kissed him, she was ready to throw conscience to the winds and sleep with him. He saw her as a quick pickup, a one-night stand.

Anger fired her voice. "No, thanks." She reached for the door handle.

"Mila, we have to talk," he said.

"Talk? Is that what you have in mind, Brett?" She gave an ironic laugh. "I've done all the 'talking' I'm going to. Thanks for dinner."

She opened the door and got out swiftly. He got out his own door and came after her. "What's the matter? Why are you suddenly acting like this?"

She said the first thing that came into her mind, anything to get away. "This is the way I always act. Kiss and run."

He took her arm and pulled her to a stop. "A creature of moods, huh?" He smiled, trying to put a good face on it. "Maybe you're right. It's a little premature for the particular mood we were in. I really should . . ." He stopped and glanced at his watch.

She felt a blinding fury, and hurried on toward the hotel door. "If you hurry, she should still be there. She said an hour."

"What?"

"Bonnie will be at the club for an hour. Maybe *she'll* be in the mood. Goodbye, Brett."

She opened the door and fled into the hotel. She heard the echo of some educated profanity as the door closed behind her. In her room, she flung off her clothes and had a shower, to wash away the anger and the feeling of being soiled. She didn't even have the consolation of being able to say it was his fault. She had led him on—that was what it amounted to. No wonder he thought she was willing to sleep with him. One kiss and she'd melted in his arms.

"No better than she should be." That was the way her mother described women who behaved as she'd behaved that night. It had always seemed a vague sort of an insult to Mila. Who *was* "better than she should be"? "Worse than she should be"—that made sense.

She got out of the shower and dried herself roughly, pulling the towel across her shoulders and legs till the skin was pink. As she lay in bed, she tried to understand why she was so furious. Brett had behaved like a perfect gentleman all evening. He had apologized, offered to help, he had accepted total responsibility for the accident. So why was she mad as a hornet? At last she accepted the truth. It wasn't his lovemaking that annoyed her. She had enjoyed it thoroughly. She could even accept that he asked her to his house for the night, as long as he was willing to take a refusal gracefully—and he had.

No, it was the quick peek at his watch, and the knowledge that he was going to enjoy his "mood" with Bonnie Clarke that was keeping her awake. She was jealous, as he was of Rick. It was crazy to be jealous of a chance acquaintance. That was all they were to each other, and all they ever would be. A pair of chance acquaintances, whose chemistry happened to click, turning them temporarily insane. The best way to keep combustible chemicals from igniting was to keep them well separated. No problem there. They'd soon be separated by one hundred fifty miles.

That was settled, and now she'd go to sleep. But the memory of igniting chemicals kept her awake for two more hours, and left her heavy-eyed and still angry in the morning.

Chapter Six

Mila awoke groggy and grumpy in the morning. After breakfast, she phoned her mother. "Hi, Mom. I just thought I'd let you know how things are going. The man who hit Madam X is going to pay for all the repairs, so that's okay. I'll be home this afternoon."

"Home? Aren't you staying for the show, dear, it's only one more day."

"There's not much point now that you and Bob won't be coming."

"Bobbie is going to Rochester today. He got an afternoon off work especially for this. He was planning to drive you home after the Concours on Sunday."

"I didn't think he'd bother coming when Madam X isn't in the show."

"Young Healey called him. He got free tickets from somewhere, and there's one of those drag races he wants to attend tonight. Bobbie's staying with Rick, so it won't cost much. Why don't you stay on, Mila? Only one more night—you need a little vacation."

Mila bit her lip in indecision. It seemed foolish to take a bus home, when she could get a drive with Bob if she stayed one more day. The Concours d'Élégance was always interesting—all those old Duesenbergs and Packards and Mercedes, and the setting at the golf club of Oakland University was beautiful. She'd like to visit Meadow Brook Hall again, the enchanting old 120-room mansion built for John Dodge's widow in the 1920s. She could go to the drag races with Rick and Bob at night. But really what tempted her more strongly than any of these enticements was that in a town the size of Rochester, she might quite possibly bump into Brett Fletcher.

"Oh, I don't know," she said doubtfully. "It'll leave you all alone, Mom. Why don't you come with Bob?"

"You know I dreaded going worse than a trip to the dentist. Why, I was half hoping Madam X wouldn't win a prize, so I wouldn't have to go up on the stand and accept it. I'm going to Vera's cottage for the weekend." Her Aunt Vera's cottage overlooking Lake Michigan held some attraction for Mila. Isolation and wilderness had a certain appeal in her present mood. But there wouldn't be isolation. There'd be Vera's children and grandchildren, all clamoring four of them. Mila liked children, but at the time, she wanted peace and quiet more. "In fact, we're leaving at noon," her mother added.

"I wouldn't be seeing you when I got home then. Well, have a nice time. Give my love to Vera and the kids." If Bobbie was bringing the car to Rochester, she wouldn't have any way of getting to the cottage. She'd be home alone.

"I will. I wouldn't have accepted if I'd thought you meant to come home," her mother added doubtfully.

The next step would be that Mom would offer to stay home, and Mila knew she loved visiting the cottage. "In that case, I might as well stay here," she said quickly.

Her mother sounded relieved. "I don't see why not. It'll be fun. Do you have enough clean clothes? You didn't take much with you. Your nice green dress you meant to wear to that cocktail party and dinner for the Concours entries is all pressed."

"I could use a few shirts," Mila said. "Sure, you might as well send the dress, too." The mint-green sundress was her best, her fanciest dress. The only place in Rochester that would require such a dress was Bonnie Clarke's party, which Mila wasn't planning to attend. She thought it must be her subconscious giving the request.

"You'll want your light sandals, too, then, I expect."

"Yes, and the green earrings—you know, the ones like a little cluster of grapes."

"I know the ones. I'll slip everything into a bag. Oh, and you need your strapless bra and half-slip too. I'll get everything together for you. And don't worry about the money for the hotel, Mila. I've been doing my bookkeeping, and if we can hold on with the old refrigerator for another year, we'll make out without worrying about a mortgage."

"Good. What happened, did you win a lottery?"

"No, I got an offer of a job."

"A job?" Mila was surprised at the notion of her gray-haired mother who had never worked outside the house a day in her life suddenly becoming a career woman. "Doing what?"

"Selling wool and embroidery and things at the local handicraft shop. I was buying some wool for my Christmas knitting, and Annie Morin asked me if I knew anyone who might be interested in helping her out. She's getting on, you know. It would only be three days a week to start, but if I like it, it could be full time. I think I'll take it myself. I mentioned it, and Annie was in favor. Bobbie will be away at college next year, and I'm alone all day. It's lonesome," she said, not with self-pity, but simply stating a fact.

"Yes, I know it is, Mom. The job sounds great."

"I think it does. I'll tell you, Mila, I know a sight more about wool than Annie Morin does. She tried to palm me off with wool from a different lot for the sweater I'm knitting Aunt Vera—three shades lighter, anyone could see it. I believe her eyes are fading on her. And she's been promising to get me embroidery hoops for a month now, with never a sign of them. I'll be there to jog her memory. All my friends will be in to buy their supplies. I'm looking forward to it."

Mrs. Dempster sounded so happy and excited that Mila knew it was the right thing. She'd often thought her mother should do something more than keep house. A little bungalow couldn't occupy all her time. Her mother was moving on, adjusting to her widowhood. She was only fifty-four, too young to consider her life over.

"What do you think? Should I take it?"

"Yes, take it."

"I will. I'll do it," her mother said. Already she sounded happier—more sure of herself. "I'm going to call Annie this minute, before I go to the cottage. Vera will think I've gone mad."

Vera had been urging such a scheme for months, but with no real hope of being heeded. They finished their conversation, and Mila sat down to consider how life would be with this new element added. It was bound to be better for her mother, give her a new interest. Life changed. It went on, oblivious to death and heartache. Life *was* change. There would be other changes, too. Mom might even get married again at some future time. And Bobbie would be going to college. Mila was happy for her mother, but a sad sense of loss pervaded her. Her whole life—the security blanket of a close family—a father, and a mother who was always at home—was being torn apart. It had to happen sooner or later, but she wished it hadn't happened so fast, so suddenly, so—now. Now, when she already felt sore over Brett. But brooding was the worst thing to do.

She'd get out of the hotel—go down to Rick's garage and see if he'd contacted Henderson, or sent the chrome light bar to Hibernia for repair.

She enjoyed the walk. Rochester was a pleasant little town. This older portion had towering oaks, pines and maples. There was history to be read in the fine old municipal buildings, and pride in their preservation. But there was modernity, too, in the interesting shops and boutiques. It seemed like a nice place to live. Not that she was ever likely to be living there!

"Hi, doll face," Rick said when she entered his garage. He was lying flat on his back on a creeper that he'd just rolled out from under a Corvette. "Did you hear Bob's coming down for the races tonight?"

"Yes, I was just talking to Mom."

"You're welcome to tag along if you like."

"Thanks, I might do that. Are you racing?"

"Nah, I haven't had time to get the slicks put on my 'Cuda. She needs a tune-up, too. I'll be in the next race." He jumped up, rubbing his hands on a rag so covered with oil it couldn't possibly do anything but make his hands dirtier. He finished the process by rubbing his palms on the seat of his jeans. Despite his condition, he looked attractive. A certain male animal magnetism was there, in his bright eyes, in his chestnut hair that grew in a tousled cap, and most of all in his physique, which bulged under his ever-present yellow T-shirt.

"Want a coffee?" he asked.

She didn't feel up to Rick's instant coffee with artificial whitener. "I've just had breakfast, thanks. Did you get in touch with Henderson?"

"I couldn't reach him. He's never in. I don't know how the guy makes a living. No hurry—we've got a year."

"Did you send the chrome bar to Hibernia?"

"I haven't got it. Brett Fletcher wanted to have a go at it."

She came to attention. "Brett Fletcher? When . . ."

"He stopped by last night—late, about ten o'clock."

He had left her not much before ten. She remembered seeing Rick's lights on as they drove past. Was that where he was going—and she'd accused him of running to meet Bonnie?

"I was just locking up," Rick continued. "One of his factories does that kind of work, he says."

"Oh Rick, I wish you hadn't given it to him! He might wreck it."

"I didn't want to, but he insisted. He says he's paying the shot, and he didn't see why he shouldn't have a go at fixing it himself at his factory. I guess he was afraid that if a fender cost five thousand bucks, the bar might set him back another thou or so. It shouldn't cost anywhere near that, but he wouldn't take no for an answer. He . . ." Rick came to a guilty stop.

Mila looked up sharply. "He what?"

"He took the twisted fender, too. I told him it couldn't be straightened out. Even if he could get it smooth again, the paint would be all wrong. He took the owner's manual from the glove compartment as well. I told him that was irreplaceable. He said he'd be careful. Jeez, what a pain when people that don't know anything about old cars go butting in. He was bugging me about getting a repro fender for the car again.''

"But why? He knows repro parts are an automatic disqualification.''

"Don't worry. I told him no way, José. Too bad he didn't claim any insurance. The poor guy's being stung. Five thousand is a lot to pay out of your own pocket.''

An angry frown settled on Mila's face. "His pockets are plenty deep. He can afford it. He didn't say anything about this before. I don't understand what—''

"He seemed in kind of an ugly mood when he got here,'' Rick mentioned.

Mila wanted to hear more, and worded her question discreetly. "I wonder why?''

"I didn't ask, doll face. Probably woman trouble. He was alone at ten o'clock at night. I bet his date wouldn't play ball with him,'' he suggested, with a knowing look.

Mila felt an angry twisting in her heart as this truth struck home. So that was it! Brett was willing to be a perfectly generous gentleman when he thought he could charm her into spending the night with him, but if she wasn't interested in playing ball, he wasn't interested in honoring his obligations.

"How long did he stay?" she asked in a tightly controlled voice.

"A while."

"But how long?"

"I didn't think to time him. Ten minutes maybe. Why?" he asked with quickening interest.

"Oh, I was just thinking that left him plenty of time to pick up some other girl. At a club or something," she added.

"I guess a guy like Fletcher wouldn't have much trouble. But don't tell him what I said, huh?"

"Why not?"

"Are you kidding? He's got a fleet of trucks plus all the company cars. If I could get a contract from Fletcher, I could expand, hire a couple of mechanics, spend my time counting my profits and doing more interesting work. I might actually get my 'Cuda tuned up for dragging. I was real smooth with Fletcher. He's not such a bad buy, when you get to know him."

"Wrong, motor head," she said through gritted teeth. Motor head was an acceptable insult from a mechanic's daughter. In fact, it was the way Bob and Rick usually referred to each other, but her tone caused Rick to look at her doubtfully.

"What's got your pistons misfiring?" he asked.

"Brett Fletcher's a jerk. And if he wrecks the light bar from Madam X, I'll..." She could think of no fate bad enough for him. "I want you to phone him right away and demand that he send back the fender. I don't want an amateur fiddling around with that car."

"Take it easy, Mila. Jeez, is there something going on between you two—something I don't know about?"

"I think you know my opinion of him pretty well."

"Just remember he's in a position to do me a big favor. He's not happy with the guy that keeps his transportation rolling, and I dropped a hint or two. I'll call him and tell him what you said, but the fender's garbage anyway. He can't do it any harm. I buttered him up a little while he was here. I showed him a Duster I'm dropping a Hemi engine in. He had some good ideas about reinforcing the front end to take the extra weight. He knows quite a bit about that kind of stuff. Welding, stress and all that. Hey, did I tell you he gave me three free tickets for the Concours? That's why I called Bob, to offer him one. You can have the other if you want," he offered. "We're going Saturday aft_rnoon."

"I'll buy my own ticket," she said tersely, "but I'd like to go with you."

"Great, I'll give the spare to Mannie. He's always broke. Hey, you want to see something neat?" he offered, eyes shining.

"Sure, what?"

"The Duster," he said, offended that she didn't remember, or show the proper enthusiasm. "A guy from Ann Arbor drove it up for me to work on. He'd heard about me, all the way to Ann Arbor," he boasted. "I'm becoming world famous—in Michigan, I mean."

She went to view the Duster. It was a yellow two-door coupé in the process of being turned into a dragster. The interior had been gutted and a roll cage installed to protect the driver in case of accident.

"I put on the Cragar S/S rims," Rick said, pointing to the mag wheels. "I dropped this Hemi in the bay—the Duster didn't come with a Hemi, but it'll beat anything at the track once I get it dialed in."

"Great, I suppose you'll be changing the rear axle," she said, trying to show some enthusiasm, but her mind kept harking back to Brett. How could he be so deceitful, when he seemed so nice? She wondered, too, if that third ticket had been intended for her.

"For sure, and I'll put in tall spider gears, slap in positraction. She'll get twelve ninety e.t. for the quarter mile easily. Look at this," he said, and put one greasy hand on the shoulder of her white blouse as he pointed to the Hemi performance engine with the other. The awesomely broad expanse of chrome and steel, the massive valve covers with spark plug boots in them told Mila it was a Hemi engine, beloved by dragsters, but even this didn't rouse her to the heights it should have.

"Oh, Rick!" she exclaimed, looking at the imprint of his palm and four fingers on her blouse.

"Sorry, doll." He made an exaggerated grimace.

"And I haven't got any clean clothes left. What am I going to wear?"

"It'll come out. It's only grease," he said naively. "No problem. I'll give you one of my promo shirts."

She looked askance at the garish yellow shirt he was wearing himself, and didn't particularly want to be seen on the streets in a replica.

"I'm going to see if I can wash this grease out before it sets."

"Don't do me any favors," he said, offended. "They cost me five bucks each. You look as if it's gross or something. You should see the ones I turned down."

"It looks fine on you, Rick. It's just not me."

She went to the washroom and blotted at the grease with paper towels and soap, but the stain only spread. Her shirt was too wet and too dirty to wear. She'd have to wear one of Rick's promo shirts after all.

She opened the door and called to him. "Bring the smallest one you've got," she said, and fished out her five dollars to hand him through the partially closed door.

Mila pulled the shirt over her head, and as the tail came nearly down to her thighs, she tucked it into the waistband of her jeans. It was loose enough that with her own blouse beneath, her breasts weren't as much in evidence as she feared. Being a small-town school teacher, she was a little careful about what she wore in public. You couldn't go a block without meeting some of your students, or worse, their parents. Parents liked to know the lives of their impressionable youngsters were in good, respectable hands. But she wasn't likely to meet anyone she knew in Rochester, so she straightened her hair and forgot about it.

When she came out, she turned around to show Rick the shirt. "The best advertisement I've had yet," he said with a smile. "If you don't have customers breaking down my door, I'll be a ring-tailed raccoon.

It'd be robbery for you to pay me for being a walking billboard for the garage. Here, take back your five bucks,'' he said, and stuffed it into her fingers.

"No, really, I'm glad to pay."

"Your money's no good around here, angel eyes."

"Thanks, Rick," she said, and on impulse, reached up and kissed his cheek.

She thought his look of surprise was at this innovation in their relationship. She'd never kissed Rick before, and only did it from friendship now. "What's the matter?" she asked.

"Nothing," he said, looking down at her. "It's just Fletcher. Stay cool."

She turned around and saw Brett standing in the doorway staring at them, and her heart seemed to stop beating, just before it went into a convulsed flutter. He didn't look like the deceitful man she was fast convincing herself he was. He just looked like himself, like the man she had found so enchanting last night. Tall and suave, and once again in a business suit that set off his lean charms so devastatingly that she found herself falling under his spell, even while she tried to hate him. There was no furious glitter in his eyes, no rigid shoulders, or other marks of rampant jealousy. He just stood still, watching them with quiet intensity. Why wasn't he jealous of Rick now, when he'd actually seen her kissing him? It was all a charade, his saying that last night. He looked thoughtful, perhaps a little disconcerted, but made a rapid recovery.

"Am I intruding?" he asked, and walked forward before anyone had time to answer him.

Mila stiffened in hostility, but Rick was pacing forward, hand outstretched in welcome like an eager salesman. "Mr. Fletcher, nice to see you again. I was just showing Mila the Duster I showed you last night."

"Is *that* what you were doing? It looked like something else to me," he said, shooting a quick, accusing glance at Mila. "Let's make clear for the lady's benefit that you showed me the car in a less amorous manner last night, Rick." To Mila he added, "I didn't know you were interested in drag racing."

"There are lots of things you don't know about me," she snapped. "And a few things you don't know about antique cars either. I hope you've returned the pieces of Madam X you took away last night."

"No, as a matter of fact I've come back for more pieces. The hardware that holds the chrome bar on might have to be replated, along with the bar, if it's been marred in the accident. You'll notice I've been doing my homework on showing cars, and learned the importance of details."

"A chromed bolt isn't as likely to lose points as a reproduced fender," she pointed out. "I was just telling Rick to call you to bring back the fender. How *dare* you . . ."

Brett blinked in astonishment at this unexpected attack. "I was trying to help," he said simply.

"You've helped just about enough, Mr. Fletcher," she shot back angrily. "Don't think you're going to palm me off with a cheap and shoddy replacement fender, because you're not."

His brows lowered, and the glitter that jealousy had failed to cause glowed in his navy-blue eyes now. His lips thinned, but before he could speak, Rick interfered. "Hey, you guys, let's lighten up here. No harm done."

"That's a matter of opinion," Mila said, and stalked off to wait for Rick in his office. She was trembling. Her whole insides were shaking, which was a perfectly ridiculous reaction to Brett's having removed a few broken pieces from her car. She reminded herself he was trying to chisel out of his bargain, but even that wasn't the reason she was so furious, and she knew it. She was angry because he'd lied. He'd said he was jealous, and he wasn't. He didn't bat an eye when she kissed Rick. If he loved her even a little, he would have been jealous. And if she loved him less, she would be less mad, too. That was it then, she had actually fallen in love in the space of two nights and one day.

When had it happened? It certainly wasn't a case of love at first sight, or even second. You didn't fall in love with a man who called you a kid. You didn't fall in love with a man who pushed you in a pool. No, who you fell in love with was a man who took you out to dinner and was a charming, thoughtful companion. It was love at third sight, that's what it was. But it was back to hate at fourth.

She peered through the office door and saw Rick making his pitch to Brett, trying to get the contract for keeping his vehicles in repair. He was pointing out the various features of his shop, the hoist and other me-

chanical marvels he'd accumulated over the years.
Rick was a good mechanic; she'd told Brett so herself. She wished him well, but there was no way she
would help. In fact, the best thing she could do was
disappear. She picked up her purse and slipped quietly out the office door that led to the gas pumps. She
noticed Brett's Porsche had been repaired. It was
parked at the side of the garage.

She turned the corner so the men couldn't see her if
they happened to look out the window, and found
herself on an abandoned railroad track, heading away
from the business section of town. To the west was a
park with a fountain and she crossed the street to sit
on one of the pretty wrought-iron benches there. This
visit to Rochester was supposed to be fun, a little vacation, and here she sat roasting to death on a park
bench, like a retired pensioner waiting for—what? For
noon hour, so she could eat some food she didn't
want? For Bob's arrival with the green dress that she
wouldn't be wearing? For the drag race that would be
dusty and noisy and no real fun for her?

Or would she just forget the race and stay in her
room, thinking about the party that Brett was at
without her? That would be a real ball, a fitting end to
a hellish visit that had brought nothing but sorrow.
He'd be dancing with Bonnie Clarke, holding that
glamorous, leggy blonde in his arms, probably taking
her out into the garden for a walk. She didn't think
he'd have much trouble putting Bonnie in the mood.
The woman's eyes practically devoured him. His
smooth black hair that glinted with blue under lights,

his darkly dangerous eyes and that lean body with broad shoulders. Mr. Three Piece Suit, Rick called him, but it was just resentment of the trappings of success.

Mila drew a weary sigh and glanced toward the street. Might as well go back to the hotel and make use of the pool. The day was warm, and a pool an unaccustomed luxury for her. She had just risen when she saw a low-slung silver sports car drive by, slowly, as though looking for someone. Brett? Yes, it was the Porsche, and who else would he be looking for in this vicinity but her? She sat down again and edged back on the bench to hide behind a white-leaved dogwood bush. The car picked up speed and dashed away around a corner. He hadn't seen her, and that made her sad, too. What could he have wanted? Was he going to apologize?

Maybe he was going to invite her to the party again. Maybe Rick had mentioned that she was staying over and ... And Brett Fletcher, that arrogant corporation chief, was going to come begging to her for a date? Not likely! She gazed at the fountain. Droplets of water sprinkled from the mouths of concrete dolphins that stood playfully on their tails. Sun shone through the individual droplets, suspended for a second in the air, turning them into a shower of iridescent diamonds. Why did all the wonderful miracles of nature have to be so evanescent?

She leaned forward, looking at the diamond droplets of water splashing into the fountain, to be swallowed up by the brackish water below. Just like life.

Her wistful face was dappled by shafts of light that penetrated the trees overhead. Spots of burnished copper were reflected on her titian hair and warmed her shoulders as she sat, motionless as the concrete dolphins, thinking her gloomy thoughts.

The approaching footsteps were swallowed up by the grass. She didn't hear Brett approach, didn't know he had found her until he was suddenly there, a shadow looming on the lawn, blocking the sun and robbing the falling water of its magic. She assumed it was one of the old people who occupied the other benches. She looked up, ready to smile and move graciously aside to make room for the intruder. The incipient smile turned to ice when she saw who it was. A scowl pulled Brett's lips into a thin line.

"More of your kiss-and-run tactics, Mila?" he asked sardonically.

Her answer was equally rude. "What do you want?" she asked gruffly. She stared at him, as he was staring at her. He, too, was dappled by the sun, and this gave him an insubstantial aura, as though he might disappear without warning. He had removed his jacket, and carried it slung over his shoulder. His broad frame was revealed, tapering to a flat stomach and narrow hips. He held a brown bag in his hand, but flung it on the bench before speaking.

"I want you to take off that obscene T-shirt," he snapped.

"Obscene?" She looked at him, incredulous, then gave a mocking laugh. "Only you would find it obscene."

The summer sun, or perhaps it was only anger, made him hot, and he jerked at his collar, opening it and pulling his tie askew. "It's vulgar, and you know it perfectly well. What it denotes is obscene. If using lo—friendship for financial gain isn't obscene, I don't know what is."

"I don't know what you're talking about."

"Don't you?" he asked, and leaned menacingly over her, resting his hands on the backrest of the bench. His face was so close she could touch it. It was burning with anger. She could feel the warmth of his breath, and see the nervous working of his jaw. Where he had pulled his collar open, a triangle of brown chest with a tuft of black hair peeked out. Something in her began to soften at the sight, and the thoughts it caused to dart into her head. "You must think I'm still wet behind the ears. Now I understand why you were so amiable last night, and so quick to run when I fell for it. If you think you're going to romance me into giving Healey the contract for my fleet with a couple of kisses, you're out to lunch."

It took her a moment to make any sense of this charge. The only "financial gain" she could think of was what Rick had said—that her wearing the shirt would bring business to the garage. What was Brett implying, anyway? That she let him kiss her last night so he'd give Rick the contract? And that she'd refused to go home with him because she was in love with Rick? He was practically accusing her of prostitution. Her heart pounded, sending the blood flooding hotly through her veins, and her eyes sparkled dangerously. "I don't buy favors for anyone with my body, Mr. Fletcher. The favor doesn't exist that could induce me to go to bed with you. I wouldn't sleep with you if you promised to give me Fletcher Enterprises on a platter. As to paying for favors, I notice you weren't so eager to fork over the five thousand for Madam X once I turned down your offer of hospitality! You were so anxious to foist a cheap home-made repair job on me you even went to steal the fender before you kept your date with Bonnie Clarke."

He looked blank at these charges, but had soon figured them out. "I didn't have a date with Bonnie Clarke! And I didn't steal the fender. I borrowed it, for a very good reason."

"Yes, for the good reason that you don't want to pay for a new one. You'd better get it back. And you'd better not destroy that chrome bar, or you'll have to replace it, too. How dare you take those priceless pieces away, to have some bumbling technician..."

"I don't hire bumbling technicians. My man is the best in the field. I make fine surgical equipment as well as ball bearings. He straightened out the piece and re-chromed it to factory specs."

"Well, he needn't waste his time straightening out the fender, because not even your geniuses are going to match the patina of a paint job that's over fifty years old."

"Then you shouldn't have any objection to my taking it," he retaliated.

As this was perfectly true, she could do no more than toss her head and glare. "Did you come here to tell me that?" she demanded.

"No, and I didn't come here to be insulted, either. You've just called me a—a *pervert*," he charged, unhappy with the word, but no better one occurred to him. "You implied I was welching on our bargain because you wouldn't play ball."

"That's the way it looked to me."

"Then you're blind as a bat. I'll return the precious crumpled fender, and the chrome bar, and I'll pay for the replacement from Henderson as I always intended to, without any bodily favors from you. I'm not that hard up for women that I have to buy them," he sneered. He straightened up, and ran his dark eyes over her small body. "Personally, I think you overestimate your charms. Five thousand is a bit steep for a one-night stand."

She jumped to her feet, and in a blinding flash of fury, she lashed out at him. Her hand whipped through the air, landing on his cheek with a loud whack. Not anticipating such violence, he teetered precariously. For one awful minute Mila thought he was going to tumble into the fountain. She watched in horror as his body leaned over it, and instinctively reached out to pull him back.

He shook her off and straightened up. She knew he was suppressing an urge to return that slap. His nostrils were pinched and his face flushed, his hands were clenched into fists with the effort. "Children solve

their problems by physical violence, Mila. Grow up,"
he said, and turned on his heel to stalk back to his car.

She was still standing by the fountain, looking
helplessly after him when he ground the gears of his
Porsche and took off. She felt weak, almost nau-
seated. It was as if she'd just been kicked in the stomach. She straggled to the bench and sat down. The
brown bag Brett had brought was still on the bench,
and she picked it up listlessly. It was just an ordinary
brown paper bag—his lunch? The contents felt soft.
She opened the bag and saw a white cotton-knit T-
shirt. It had something printed on it, and as a T-shirt
wasn't in any way private, she pulled it out to read the
inscription. Fletcher Team Mate, it said, like the ones
she'd seen around town. She noticed it was a small
size.

Why had he brought it here? Was it for her? She
looked at the yellow shirt she wore, Rick's promo.
Obscene, Brett had called it. So he didn't like that she
wore a shirt proclaiming to the town her familiarity
with Rick. That was none of his darned business. Yet
she was more intrigued than annoyed by Brett's inter-
ference, because it was beginning to look like jealousy. He said he hadn't come to tell her why he'd
taken the chrome bar and fender, so why had he
come? To give her the T-shirt? A man didn't come
looking like a thundercloud if that was his playful er-
rand. Of course she'd been pretty rude, right from the
start. Maybe if she'd been more pleasant... It looked
as if he was trying to help; he *was* having his specialist
take time to fix up the chrome bar.

He must have seen her when he drove past the first time, and just driven around looking for a place to park. What would have happened if she'd behaved differently? Would he have softly said that he didn't want her wearing any shirt but his? That he wanted her for a member of the Brett Fletcher team? She lifted the soft white shirt and buried her face in it. She felt like crying, but a public park wasn't the place for that. She walked slowly through the park back to the hotel.

A big wicker basket of fruit wrapped in cellophane had been put on the dresser during her absence. Oranges, grapes, peaches, pears, bananas, kiwis, a pomegranate. She rushed toward it, full of excitement, and hastily pulled out the card to read, sure it was from Brett. A smile lit her face as she tore open the envelope. This was a good excuse to call him. The little white square said "Compliments of the Management," and her joy vanished. Jack Orr had sent it, because he thought she was a friend of the illustrious Mr. Fletcher.

She dropped the card in the wastebasket, and didn't even bother opening the basket of fruit. Stupid manager, what did he think she wanted with a big basket of fruit? It would feed an army. Why couldn't he have sent flowers, if he wanted to honor Brett's friend? And why was she being such an ungrateful wretch? It was unlike her. She went to the phone and called the manager to thank him.

"My pleasure, Miss Dempster. Any friend of Brett Fletcher is a friend of the hotel. We want you to feel welcome. Brett sends a lot of business our way. Of course he has his own guesthouse, but it only houses two, and he often has more men visiting the plant. And there are the conventions—an annual event. You might just mention to him that you enjoyed the fruit.''

"I'll be sure to," she said uncomfortably, and hung up. Sure I will, if I ever happen to see him again, she muttered to herself.

She glanced in the mirror and saw a sulky pout staring back at her. A child, Brett had called her, and she looked like one. A thoroughly bad-tempered child. Grow up, he had said. She was tired of being grown up. Being grown up was the pits. Grown-ups fell in love and got their hearts smashed to smithereens. Grown-ups had to worry about money, about paying bills, about missing parties. Surely that was why Brett had come to the park, to ask her to the party again? Her head ached. It felt as if a screw was being driven into her temple.

Maybe she should phone Brett... And say what? He had accused her of trying to finagle a job for Rick by being nice to him. Maybe she should phone and tell him to stuff his T-shirt down his throat. She wasn't the only one who had acted like a dumb kid. He was pretty childish himself, if it came down to that. People did tend to behave childishly when they were afraid. Her own mother had practically regressed to infancy when Dad died. She used to ask Bobbie and Mila what she should buy for dinner, and whether she should go shopping or to a movie, and all types of silly things she never asked them before. It was as if she were adrift, with no anchor, and no beacon to steer her course.

Was Brett afraid, too? Was that why he went leaping from one unfounded assumption to another, with all the agility of a mountain goat?

Mila felt like someone was turning the screw in her temple. She felt fevered and sick and sore all over. She felt hungry, too, but the very sight of all that beautiful fruit made her realize the impossibility of forcing food past the blockage in her throat. Aspirin—she needed aspirin. Even that small pill felt like a rock when she swallowed it. She looked at the bed, all neatly made up again, and walked slowly toward it. She kicked off her shoes, but before she lay down she got the white T-shirt from the bag and took it to bed with her, fondling it in her fingers like a security blanket. The aspirins made her sleepy.

But she didn't sleep, or even try to. She just lay quietly, thinking of what might have been. She wondered what Brett was doing. At least he had his work to distract him.

But in the office of the president of Fletcher Enterprises, very little work was being done. The chief executive paced the floor, rubbing the back of his neck and cursing himself for being an idiot. His personal problems put out of his mind that he was supposed to send glasses for Bonnie's party. After all his frantic dashing around to help Mila, she had the temerity to accuse him of that—welching because she wouldn't... Damnation, but she was infuriating.

At eleven o'clock, Harvey Clarke dropped in to remind Brett that he hadn't sent the glasses for the party.

Harvey noticed his boss's distracted mood. "You *will* be coming, I hope?" he asked.

"Of course," Brett answered unenthusiastically.

"It'll be a great do. Bonnie hired a band from Pontiac. We're going to dance out on the patio, beside the pool."

"That sounds fine, Harvey. Who are you taking?" Brett asked, stirring himself to show some interest.

"I didn't bother getting a date. I'm Bonnie's host, I'll just circulate—an extra man is always handy at these things."

Brett's eyes narrowed, and he looked at Harvey Clarke with a speculative gleam. "I have a friend I'd like to ask. She needs a date. Since you don't have one..."

"Of course. I'd be happy to oblige, Brett. Anyone I know?"

"You met her last night," Brett said.

"Why don't you ask her yourself?"

"She's already turned me down. Don't tell her this is my idea. Here, I'll give you her number. She'll say no, but if you insist—well, I don't have to tell the town's top bachelor how to convince a lady, do I?"

Flattered at this outrageous praise, Harvey smiled and took down the name and number.

Chapter Seven

The jangling of the phone was an unwelcome interruption to Mila, till the idea took hold that it was
Brett. She hurried across the room and said, "Hello,"
in a light, hopeful voice.

"Miss Dempster—Mila Dempster?"

She didn't recognize the voice, though it sounded
vaguely familiar. Really all she noticed was that it
wasn't Brett Fletcher, and her hopes evaporated.
"Yes, speaking."

"This is Harvey Clarke. We met last evening at the
Lobster Shack."

"Harvey Clarke," she repeated dumbly. Now what
in the devil did he want with her? "Yes, of course I
remember."

"Good. How are you?"

"I'm fine."

"I happened to see you downtown this morning, and as you're still in town, I'm calling to see if I can't persuade you to come to our little party tonight. My sister mentioned it to you, perhaps you remember."

Mila had hardly thought of anything else for half the night, but in all her imagining it had never occurred to her that Harvey Clarke might ask her as his date. It came as such a shock that she wanted to think about it for a few minutes before deciding. "Well, I don't know," she said hesitantly. But she knew that every fiber of her being was aching to go. She knew that Bob was bringing her best dress to Rochester, and that heart and mind would be at the party, wherever her body spent the evening.

"Please come. We'd love to have you. The fact is, my date canceled on me at the last minute, and here I am, without a date for my own party. We're having a dance outdoors and midnight dinner."

It sounded gloriously romantic. She pictured a fat yellow moon hanging low over treetops, with soft music playing. She could see herself dancing—but not with Harvey Clarke, who was about as exciting as vanilla ice cream. She wouldn't have every dance with Harvey, either. The irony of showing up with Bonnie's brother appealed to her sense of humor. Wouldn't Brett's eyes open up if she waltzed in on Harvey's arm! Soon she had mentally revised it to *when* she waltzed in.

"It sounds fabulous. I hate to think of you being without a date for your own party," she said, still not certain she could go through with it.

"Then you'll come," he assumed.

"Yes, all right. How nice of you to ask me. I guess you know where I'm staying, as you called me here at the hotel."

"Yes."

"How did you happen to know that?" she asked suspiciously.

"Why, you told us last night," he answered easily. He had been coached well.

"Oh, of course," she said, though she wasn't sure she had told him. Still, it was hardly a memorable detail—she'd probably mentioned it.

"Is eight o'clock all right?"

"Eight's fine, Harvey."

"I don't know if I told you it's kind of a fancy party. I don't mean evening gowns or anything, but the ladies will be dressed up."

"Of course. Kind of you to mention it."

"I know you women like to be in style."

"I'll do my best," she promised.

When she hung up, the lump in her throat had miraculously vanished, to be replaced by a feverish excitement singing in her veins. The fruit suddenly looked delicious. She removed the yellow cellophane and selected an orange that was nearly as big as a cantaloupe. She sat at the window and ate it, section by section, savoring every juicy morsel. The main street of Rochester was spread below her, but her eyes didn't register the passing flow of traffic. What she saw was a dance floor under the stars, on which she spun in dizzying circles with Brett's arms around her. Not once during the twenty minutes she sat there did she so much as think of Harvey Clarke.

When Mila had finished eating, she rose and shook away the daydreams. Now, what had to be done for the party? It wasn't quite noon yet, and too early to begin preparations, even if her outfit had been here. She had more than eight hours to fill in. For some reason that she didn't care to examine too closely, she decided to stay away from Rick's garage. She'd do what she was supposed to be doing—enjoy herself, have a little vacation.

First she had a long, leisurely sun bath, followed by a dip in the pool. Next she put on her blue cotton dress and ate a civilized lunch of fruit salad and cottage cheese in the hotel dining lounge. After lunch she went for a stroll through the small town, looking at the stores and boutiques, buying nothing except a chocolate soda at a coffee shop when she began to feel warm. Every time a Fletcher Team Mate shirt went by, she felt a tug of attraction, as if she *were* a part of the team.

At four-thirty, she went back to the hotel, and before five, her brother called from the lobby. She gave Bob her room number and he came right up. Bob Dempster was a six-foot young man with the same reddish hair as his sister. Unlike Mila, he had a healthy dose of freckles. He wore jeans and a blue sport shirt.

"Hi, Sis. Too bad about Madam X" was his greeting.

"I'm so sorry I could cry."

"It's not your fault. As long as the guy's willing to pay, let's not worry about it. You heard about Mom's job?"

"She told me. I think it's a good idea, don't you?"

"Just what she needs. We should encourage her to buy Annie Morin out next year, when we sell Madam X. Annie's getting too old, and the shop does a good business. Mom would be happy as a lark, surrounded by all that wool and stuff. Did Rick tell you he got free tickets for the show tomorrow?"

"Yes, he did," she said briefly.

"I'm really looking forward to the drag races tonight. Are you coming with us?"

"No, I have a date, but I wouldn't mind joining you guys for dinner first."

"Who are you going out with?" Bob asked, surprised.

"Just a man I met."

"Not that jerk who hit Madam X?" he asked swiftly.

"No, not him."

"Where'd you meet this man? You shouldn't run around with strangers, Sis."

"He's not a stranger. He's a very respectable businessman that I was formally introduced to. We're going to a high-class party, so you needn't worry that I'll get in any trouble."

"I guess you know what you're doing. Let's go pick up Rick. I'm starved. Hey, where'd you get the basket of fruit?"

"The manager sent it up to me."

"Why?"

"Small-town hospitality," she parried. "Help yourself."

Bob was young enough to accept this unlikely generosity without embarrassing questions. "Thanks." He chose an apple, and munched it while they drove down to Rick's garage.

Bob had to see Madam X before doing anything else, but soon Rick showed him the Duster, and the name of Brett Fletcher was forgotten. It was half an hour before they all went out for a pizza, and six-thirty when Mila returned to the hotel. It was finally time to get ready for the party.

She made careful preparations, took a leisurely soak in a scented bath, then she arranged her hair. For this special occasion she pulled it up loosely behind, with curls falling forward over her ears. The dangling earrings, like miniature clusters of grapes, bounced playfully against her cheeks. She applied eye shadow to enhance the sea green of her eyes, and finally slipped into the sundress. It plunged to a daring V in front and swirled out in a full, flared skirt. Her sandals had very high heels. As she turned in front of the mirror, the swish of silk against her nylon-clad legs felt as if she were already dancing.

She stood back to assess the overall effect, and was satisfied that Brett Fletcher wouldn't accuse her of being a child tonight. She looked as pretty as Bonnie Clarke. Not as glamorous or sophisticated maybe, but Brett didn't express any specific love of sophistication. Being grown up had its compensations, she decided, as she waited on pins and needles for Harvey's call.

He arrived promptly at eight, and she went down to the lobby. The widening of his eyes and the light of approval glowing in them told her she looked good. "I hardly recognized you," he said. "You look... different."

"You warned me your party was a fancy affair."

"I hope you don't mind going early. It officially starts at eight, which means eight-thirty or nine, but Bonnie wants me to be there beforehand."

"Of course." She smiled, but having to spend half an hour alone with Bonnie and Harvey was a bad start to the evening.

Harvey drove out the same road she had traveled with Brett the night before. He pulled in at the driveway of a lovely old stone house, set behind spacious lawns. Mila was happy to see there were already half a dozen cars parked in the circular driveway. She noticed at a glance that Brett's Porsche wasn't one of them, and was sorry. She wanted to see his face when she came in on Harvey's arm.

A small group had formed in the living room and were having drinks. Bonnie was busy playing hostess. Her pale blond hair was drawn behind one ear, held with a white silk gardenia. She was dressed in black again, a close-fitting dress that showed off her svelte figure and looked very sophisticated against her golden tan. She advanced at once to greet this new guest.

"Mila, how nice to see you again. A lovely surprise. I'm so glad you could stay over for the party." Her words were gracious, but a curious light flickered in her eyes. They were slate-gray eyes, as cold as wellwater.

"It was kind of you to ask me. What a beautiful house, Bonnie. You must love living here." The room they sat in was large and impressive, with a baby grand piano occupying the place of honor at the front window. Old oil paintings in heavy gilt frames showed scenes of nature. The furnishings were ornately carved, and there were Persian carpets underfoot. The carpets were well worn. Old money, Mila thought.

"I was born and raised here. I can't imagine living anywhere else. This stretch of road is quite historical. The houses were built by the founding fathers of Rochester. One of my ancestors built this house in the nineteenth century. They don't build houses on this scale nowadays. The location is ideal, too, close to all our old friends. Brett lives just down the road."

"Yes, he showed me his house," Mila retaliated demurely.

"I know." Bonnie smiled politely, but triumphantly. "What can I get you to drink, Mila?"

"A spritzer will be fine."

"Harvey, you'll take care of the bar while I introduce Mila around?"

Mila was introduced to the other guests. Some of them worked for Fletcher Enterprises, some were neighbors, and others were Bonnie's artistic friends. From what Mila could figure out, Bonnie didn't have a date. As Bonnie more than once wondered aloud what could be keeping Brett, Mila took the idea Brett was her escort. All the guests were polite and friendly, and not overly curious what this one outsider was doing in their midst. Mila felt out of place when the talk turned to local matters—a charity affair to raise funds for the symphony, a street fair that was apparently an annual event, an Art 'n' Apples Festival for the autumn. It sounded like a cultured and lively little town. Other guests arrived, and the hostess made them welcome.

During a lull, Bonnie came to sit beside Mila. "What brings you to Rochester, Mila? Are you staying long?" she asked. Her tone was casual, but again her eyes betrayed more than a passing interest.

"I'm here for the car show. I'll be leaving tomorrow."

"You're that interested in old cars, are you? A strange hobby for a young girl."

That thoughtless "girl" stung, since Bonnie couldn't be more than thirty herself. "My mother was invited to show an antique car she owns. I brought it over to be prepped for the show. Mother was planning to come for the show on Sunday, but I had an accident and we won't be showing after all."

"What a pity," Bonnie said, with some evidence of real feeling, but she wasn't curious enough to even ask what kind of car it was. She asked no questions, which Mila interpreted to mean Brett hadn't told her about the accident. This being the case, Mila didn't add any details. A party hardly seemed the place for repining.

"It wasn't serious. We'll show it next year instead."

"How did you happen to meet Brett? Or did you know him before? I've never heard him mention you."

"I didn't know him before," Mila admitted, and left Bonnie to reach her own conclusion.

Bonnie apparently concluded that a "girl" who would be leaving town the next day was no threat, as she left her alone after that. When a good-sized crowd had assembled, the party moved outside, where a small group of musicians were tuning up, and still Brett hadn't come. Harvey asked Mila to dance, and they moved to the patio, which surrounded a kidney-shaped pool. Japanese lanterns of red and blue and yellow were strung around it, bobbing in the soft breeze, and off to one side chairs and tables were ranged to hold the nondancers. Candles flickered in glass lamps at the tables, and floated in plastic flower holders in the pool, creating a fairy-tale atmosphere. The weather couldn't have been finer. It was a black velvet night, with a big white moon and a million stars. A soft breeze stirred the leaves overhead, whispering tantalizing promises. It was even more romantic than Mila had imagined, but amidst strangers, there was some charm lacking.

Harvey was an adequate dancer and tried to make her comfortable. He asked her about her work, and told her a little about his. She heard again that Brett had bought Harvey's father's business when he had died. It had been floundering, and needed an injection of capital that Harvey apparently didn't have. "The only way we could have held on was by selling the house, and it means so much to Bonnie that I didn't like to do that. We own it jointly."

"But when you marry—I mean you probably won't both want to live in it after you're married."

"We'll see," Harvey said vaguely. "I know Bonnie won't ever move far from this part of Rochester."

Mila thought about this hint, and soon concluded that Bonnie's hope was to move down the road to Brett's house. That was probably why she'd asked him to buy it. And Bonnie would make an entirely suitable wife for the town's most prominent executive. She was a native of Rochester, she knew everyone and she was active in all the local affairs. She moved graciously amongst her guests now—half of them Brett's employees. She was from the proper class, the right age and very attractive. Of course Bonnie wanted to marry Brett. Why wouldn't she? The only question was why she hadn't succeeded before now. No, there was one other question. Why had Harvey asked Mila to this party? Between him and Bonnie, they must have been able to scrounge up a date.

"Grade five, huh?" Harvey was saying. Good Lord, she'd lost track of the conversation entirely. But Harvey didn't seem to notice. "I remember my grade-five teacher. Old Miss MacPherson, a regular tartar.

She used to keep us in an hour after school just for chewing gum. Do they still give detentions, Mila?''

"Oh sure, but never on Friday. That's the day all the teachers want to get away early for the weekend."

She kept glancing toward the doorway of the living room, from which newly arrived guests occasionally joined the dance. It was nine-thirty, and still Brett hadn't come. She danced with a few other men, and found herself answering the same questions over and over. Where was she from, what was she doing in Rochester, what did she do for a living, usually followed by the trite compliment that her partner never had such a pretty teacher when he was in school. And finally they asked how she liked their little town. Then it was her turn to pose the polite questions.

By ten, she was pondering how she could make the evening more amusing. She'd say she was from Timbuktu, or Siberia, or Hollywood. She was a porno star, and she thought Rochester was the pits. But of course she didn't do it. She just kept dancing and talking, and looking at the door.

And after all her watching and waiting, she didn't see Brett when he arrived. At the end of one set, she went to the table to rest and have some wine and some shrimp canapés. Harvey sat with her, well back from the dance floor, with two tables in front of them. When the music resumed, a throng of people went to the patio. The band was playing "Moonlight and Roses." All the music had been of that old-fashioned kind, but it suited the setting. She noticed Bonnie in the crowd, dancing. Her hair gleamed like moonlight as she smiled up at the man she was dancing with. All Mila could see through the crowd was his sleeve, a light sleeve wrapped around Bonnie's black dress. Then the intervening couple moved, and she saw that the man was Brett.

His smiling face turned to blue and red and gold as he danced, smiling lovingly at Bonnie. He must find her good company. He looked happy—maybe it was love that gave him that special air. He looked alert, tense—what was it that told her he was excited? It was the way he moved, rather quickly across the densely packed floor, taking little heed of the other dancers. There—he just bumped the couple beside him. Now he was stopping to apologize, looking around. How handsome he looked—the shape of his head, the hair growing in rigidly straight sideburns. Now he was waving to some table near the patio, looking around again.

Coming to this party suddenly seemed a terrible idea. He'd know why she'd come—chasing him. That's what it amounted to, and after he'd insulted her. He'd think she didn't have an ounce of pride in her whole body, going out with Harvey when she hardly knew him. She must be mad to have come. There—he was dancing again. Thank goodness he hadn't seen her. She breathed a sigh of relief and sipped her spritzer.

"There's Brett. He was late enough. I hope there wasn't any trouble at the plant," Harvey said worriedly. "I'd better ask him."

Before she could stop him he was up, walking toward the patio. She wanted to flee, to push her way through the hedge and run home. But the Clarkes's house was out on the edge of town, too far to walk home in high-heeled sandals. She could go in and call a taxi—except to get in she'd have to pass Brett. Something very much like panic was rising in her as she sat, staring at the patio.

She watched as Harvey approached his sister and Brett. They stopped dancing and began talking to him. Harvey pointed to his table, where Mila sat numb with embarrassment. They were coming toward it, all of them, Bonnie, too. Oh God, if she could only melt and disappear into the grass. What would he do? What would he say? Most important of all, what would he think of her?

"Hello, Mila. This is a surprise," he said blandly, and shook her hand. But he didn't look surprised, or mad or happy or anything.

"Good evening." Her voice sounded weak. It sounded like a little girl's timid squeak. Grow up! "Working late?" she asked, in a firmer tone, as cold and detached as his. "Harvey was afraid there was trouble at the plant."

"No, no trouble. I had some personal business to take care of. The night's young, Bonnie's parties go on till dawn. May we join you?"

"Of course," she murmured.

Bonnie smiled politely and said, "Harvey, how about getting Brett something to drink? The usual, Brett?"

THE INFAMOUS MADAM X

"I'd prefer a beer, if you have any."

"Good idea. I'll have the same, Harvey. Is your drink all right, Mila?"

"I'm fine."

Brett and Bonnie sat side by side, and an uncomfortable silence fell on the group. "So you decided to stay after all," Brett said, after a moment.

"My brother came for the Concours. I'll be going home with him tomorrow after the show," she explained.

"Mila had planned to show her mother's old car, but she had an accident en route," Bonnie explained.

"So I hear." Brett nodded.

"Will you be one of the judges, Brett?" Bonnie asked.

"No, no. I don't know much about antique cars. They have experts for that job."

"I just thought that since it takes place here in Rochester, they'd probably snared you for the job."

Apparently Brett was very active in the community—and Bonnie knew all about it. She went on mentioning other local events and committees Brett had been instrumental in setting up. In many cases, she was also a member of the relevant committee. It was obvious they'd been close friends for years; they had a great deal in common. As Mila sat quietly, saying very little, she got the feeling she was listening to a husband and wife.

"Remember the time..." and "We really must..." and "Did you hear about Laura and Ted?" They made a striking couple, Bonnie blondly beautiful and

Brett darkly handsome. Like a husband, Brett let
Bonnie carry the burden of conversation. It was interesting to watch her scratch around for verbal offer-
ings to present him. Mila noticed, after a moment,
that Brett was distracted. He always answered Bonnie's openings, but his mind seemed to be elsewhere.
Mila wished she could think she was the distraction,
but really she couldn't say he paid much attention to
her, either.

He rose after a moment and said, "Excuse me, I
have to make a phone call. I'll be right back."

"I know there's some trouble at the plant, and he
doesn't want to spoil my party by discussing it," Bonnie confided, with a wifely frown as her eyes followed
Brett's retreating back. "Probably some detail of the
new welding facility he's opening. He works too hard.
But we mustn't let our problems interfere with your
enjoyment of the party, Mila."

It was a speech designed to make Mila realize she
was an interloper, that she had no real part in the lives
of these people. And it wasn't even said with malice;
Bonnie was simply stating a fact. Harvey came with
the drinks, and Bonnie carried hers away to speak to
some other guests. Mila stole a look at her watch: a
quarter to eleven. How soon could she leave? It had
been a very bad idea, coming here. Why had she
wanted to hurt Brett anyway? It was childish spite, but
she felt she'd aged a lot in one evening. She no longer
wanted to hurt him; she just wanted to get away and
start healing her own emotional wounds.

A group of dancers left the patio and stopped at their table. One of them asked her to dance, and Harvey encouraged this. Soon he followed her to the floor with another woman. On top of everything else, she was probably ruining Harvey's night. She felt like a child with her nose pressed to the windowpane, looking in at others having a good time. She made dutiful small talk with her partner, whose name was Derek.

"What a lovely spot for a party. I wonder how Bonnie got those candles to float on the water?"

"Bonnie always does her parties up to the nines. Let's investigate," Derek suggested, and they went to the edge of the pool. "Plastic lily pads, with votive candles. Ingenious," he said.

Suddenly Mila felt a hand on her back. "You're a reckless lady, tempting fate. One shove and you'd be in the pool—again."

"Oh!" She jumped back nervously into the arms of Brett Fletcher. His face loomed above her. In his eyes the reflection from lights beamed, and his arm tightened around her, drawing her against him. She stood transfixed for a silent moment, with her heart pounding so loudly he must hear it.

"Don't look so frightened." He laughed. "I won't push. Bonnie wouldn't appreciate such goings-on. Do you mind if I cut in, Derek?" he asked her partner.

"I'm not likely to refuse. You might fire me," Derek replied, and smiled himself away.

"Pulling rank on your employees, huh?" she accused. Without Mila's being aware of it, a glowing smile lit her face. She no longer felt like the outsider.

Brett had opened the window and invited her to join the party.

His arm felt warmly protective as it tightened around her waist. "Shall we dance?" he asked.

"I . . ."

"Are you going to make me hire you, to give me some influence on your decisions?" he asked playfully.

"I think your employees have gone beyond grade five."

He pulled her into his arms and they danced beneath the white moon, with the colored lights above and around them. The balmy breeze stirred the leaves, played with her hair. She thought it would feel strange, being in his arms, but there was no strangeness, only a sensation of being at home where she belonged.

"I suppose you were a little surprised to see me here," she said.

"I was delighted. Well, perhaps a little miffed that Harvey's persuasions proved more effective than mine. I've learned not to look a gift horse in the mouth. An unfortunate simile! You know what I mean—you're here—that's all that matters." His arms tightened, crushing her against his chest as they moved in time to the languorous music.

"His date couldn't make it at the last moment."

"I'm glad."

After a moment's silence she said, "You left a parcel on the bench this morning."

"Is that where it got to? It was a present for you."

"Thank you. I have it at the hotel. You've inadvertently given me another present, too—a basket of fruit. Jack Orr wanted me to mention it to you."

"You've mentioned it. I acted like an idiot this morning in the park. I'm not used to being accused of reneging on a bargain—and worse . . ." he added.

She leaned back and gazed at him. "Neither am I."

He gave a resigned smile. "We both acted rashly, leaping to wrong conclusions. Why do you suppose that happened, Mila?"

She read some special significance in the question. Why did people react with such hot and reckless disregard for plausibility? Why had she accused him of welching, and why had he assumed she was trying to manipulate him? Only some strong emotion could have blinded them so thoroughly. In her case, she suspected love was the cause, but this word hadn't been used between them. Why did men and women tiptoe around it as though it were nitroglycerin? Four little letters that could change a person's fate. "You've already told me why I did it. Childishness. I guess you're not as grown up as you think either."

He inclined his head to hers and gazed into her eyes, while a teasing smile played on his lips. "You know what I need, don't you? A teacher." Then he laughed, and spun in circles, dancing her off the edge of the patio to a stone walk.

With his arm still around her waist, he led her through a trellis archway into the privacy of a small rose garden. They could still hear the music and the chatter of the party. The lights were visible, too, but at a distance. "Why am I always apologizing to you? I thought love was never having to say you're sorry."

She heard the word "love' and her heart jumped. As they continued along the stone path toward a gazebo she rationalized with herself. He didn't mean real love. He was just joking. He didn't say "I love you."

"It was Rick's T-shirt that did it," he said. "That's why I brought you one of mine. Of course I was already knocked half-senseless to see you kissing him. It looked like a brotherly sort of a kiss, which is all that saved Healey from having a monkey wrench wrapped around his neck."

"I got grease on my blouse at the garage. He gave me the shirt to hide it."

"You two are just friends?"

"Old friends."

He stopped walking then and turned to look at her. "Old friendships can turn to love."

The image of Bonnie popped into her head. "They can, but ours didn't. Rick prefers his friends to have four wheels, preferably mag wheels."

"I noticed he's fallen into a passion over a Duster. No accounting for taste."

"You prefer Europeans yourself—the Porsche?"

"That isn't love. To tell the truth, I'm just using Madam Porsche. She's nothing but an expensive plaything for my jaded palate. I'm still a child, with a lust for toys. Maybe I'm growing up a little, I was never attracted to a teacher before."

They reached the gazebo and entered. It was enclosed to waist level by crossed wooden beams, leaving a clear view of the surroundings. Ghostly blossoms, all looking white against the black foliage, lent an eerie, unreal note. There were chairs and a table, but they went to the railing and gazed out. "Love" had suddenly sunk to "attracted." Mila considered this change. Her lips drooped unhappily. An attraction was nothing—a fleeting, insubstantial thing.

Brett lifted his hand and tilted her chin up. "Well?" he asked.

"Well what?" she asked grumpily.

"What I'm waiting to hear is whether my teacher feels any attraction for me."

"I'm not your teacher," she pouted, and turned away.

He put his hands on her shoulders and turned her back. "I know you're not mine—yet," he said, with a curious gaze. Then his head descended, and she lifted her lips for his kiss, contradicting her proud boast. The only reason she wasn't his was that he hadn't reached out and taken her. She was yearning to be claimed.

His hands moved down her arms in a sliding caress, pulling her closer. She felt a shudder at the brushing of his fingers over her flesh, as she molded herself to the firm, human wall of his body. Her arms went involuntarily around his neck. The absorbing roughness of his hair against her fingers, the deceptively soft neck that hardened as he shifted position, and his firming lips engrossed her senses. She felt herself melt helplessly into this other body that claimed and absorbed her senses.

A breeze riffled her hair as his lips moved tantalizingly over hers and his tongue demanded entry. It was futile to resist. She opened to him and felt a quiver of anticipation when his moist warmth invaded her to claim victory. A tingle ran up her back, along her limbs and shivered up her scalp, while her insides turned to mush. She was aware of nothing but the will to surrender, the passion to be claimed.

His hand left her waist, brushed up over her rib cage, where his fingers lingered an excruciating moment at the top of her dress, before plunging to garner her velvet bosom in the cup of his hand. His fingers squeezed gently, lifting, urging the breast out of her dress and his head went down to kiss the swell of white softness. The exciting brush of incipient whiskers felt roughly masculine against the cashmere smoothness of her skin. A flicker of moistness set off a trembling at her vital core. Then she felt the smooth abrasion of his teeth as he nipped at her nipple, and she emitted a groaning sigh.

The sound caused her to open her eyes, and she was surprised to see her fingers gouging into his neck. She was sure she'd leave bruises, but Brett didn't seem to notice. He looked sultry, drugged with desire. His eyes glittered a moment in the moonlight, his lower lip trembled, then he gathered her into his arms again for a long, deep kiss that sent her mind reeling off in a crazy flight to the stars. His tongue plundered her mouth, and his fingers closed over her breast in a gently fierce squeeze, while his other arm crushed her against him, till she hardly knew what she was doing.

Vaguely, she was aware of the feel of his hair and scalp under her fingers, which somehow turned to the swell of shoulder muscles bunched, then receding. The next time she paid a fleeting visit to earth, her arms were around his lean, hard waist, drawing him against her. Her hands were under his jacket, her fingers tugging at his shirt. She wanted to feel his flesh.

Then his lips were at her ear, with ragged breaths invading her head. "Not here. Come back to my place," he urged. "The guesthouse..."

"I can't." The words came spontaneously, automatically, from some secret corner of her heart.

He became still then, alert. "Why not?" He sounded surprised. "You know you want to, Mila."

"No, I don't want...that." She looked at him uncertainly. No, she didn't want that—one night in his visitors' wing, and an embarrassing parting in the morning. He might be able to put it out of his mind soon afterward, but a woman wouldn't so easily forget her first partner. For Mila, she wanted this first partner to be her last as well.

"What do you want?"

They both heard it at once, the crunch of shoes on the stone walk, and jumped apart. Brett ran his hands over his hair quickly, and stuffed his shirt into his trousers, while Mila moved back a discreet step.

"Brett, are you there?" It was Bonnie, carefully announcing her presence, in case Brett needed a minute to compose himself. Where had she learned such discretion? Not without some trial and error, surely.

"Here, in the gazebo," he called back, with an impatient look at Mila, just as Bonnie appeared around the corner.

"What on earth are you doing...? Oh, Mila! You're showing Mila the roses," Bonnie said tactfully. "Lovely, aren't they, but you can't really appreciate them in the dark. You must come back tomorrow and see them in daylight before you leave town." What an obliging girlfriend she was, to be sure. No embarrassing questions, no accusations, no recriminations. Did she not love Brett at all? If Mila had been in her shoes, she would have raised the roof.

Then Bonnie turned to Brett. Her manner was still perfectly polite, but Mila thought she detected a note of impatience under the calm. "Everyone's asking where you are, Brett. You just got here, you can't go hiding yourself away in a corner. May I borrow him, Mila? Harvey was wondering where you'd gone off to."

"We'll be along right away," Brett said.

"Do hurry," Bonnie urged, and left.

"She's right," Brett said, decisively. "I was already very late for the party. I'd better go. We'll get together later."

"When?" Mila asked—too quickly, too eagerly.

"We can't leave things like this. We have to talk."

She felt a little surge of hope. If he was willing to talk, to discuss their situation, then things weren't desperate. "I plan to leave tomorrow," she reminded him.

"But not till after the show. You'll be here all day."

"Tomorrow's Sunday. You won't be working...." she suggested.

"I'll be tied up for the first part of the day, unfortunately."

"Oh. I'm going to the Concours in the afternoon. Will you be there?"

"I can't promise. I might manage to drop around late in the afternoon."

"But I'll be leaving shortly after. Bobbie and I want to get home before dark."

"What's wrong with tonight?" he asked simply.

Her spine stiffened, and her voice when she answered was thin. "At your guest wing, you mean?"

"Anywhere you like, if you've taken an aversion to my hospitality suite, sight unseen. We'll go back to your hotel and talk."

"I came with Harvey," she reminded him.

"Harvey won't mind," he said unthinkingly.

His tone, his presuming that everyone was willing to change plans to oblige him, set her teeth on edge. "Maybe *I* mind, Brett. I'm sure it didn't occur to you, but I have some scruples, you know. Harvey brought me here, and I don't plan to go home with someone else. I don't have to kowtow to the president of Fletcher Enterprises."

He turned a winning smile on her. "No, don't be like that," he said, taking her hand and walking back toward the party. "We'll talk later. I have to mingle now. Being the president isn't all fun and games."

"You're not the host," she pointed out.

"True, but it's half a company party. I'm expected to do my duty."

"Then you mustn't disappoint Bonnie," she agreed with a mocking look.

"What am I going to do with you?" he asked, his voice a cajoling croon. He thought he had her in the palm of his hand, and it infuriated her. He shook his head and went off. When Mila went back to her table, Harvey wasn't there. He returned very soon, and she apologized for disappearing.

"I understand. Brett had a word with me," he said. "He'll be taking you home, but that doesn't mean we can't have a dance."

Her spine stiffened at this announcement. "You agreed with Brett about that, did you?"

"Oh certainly. He's the boss."

"He's not *my* boss, and you can tell him I said so." She jumped up and stalked into the house. She was outraged at the way Brett wielded his influence, telling his employees whom he'd take home. And Harvey—what kind of a man was he that he bent like a reed to his boss's demands? Didn't people have any private, personal lives in this town? Backbone, that's what they lacked, but she'd be damned if she'd jump to Brett Fletcher's tune.

She went to the phone and called a taxi. She wouldn't bother disturbing anyone by announcing her departure, but she told a maid who was fixing dinner in the kitchen that she was leaving, if anyone was wondering. Not that they'll give a hoot, she muttered to herself. She went out the front door and waited for the taxi to come.

It was just eleven o'clock. "The hotel," she said, and climbed into the back seat to review in her mind the disastrous outcome of the party, which had held such high promise.

Chapter Eight

She'd done the right thing to refuse Brett. He was arrogant, presumptuous and selfish. He thought only of himself. He knew she was going to be in town only one more day, but he couldn't rearrange his schedule to be with her. What was so important anyway? He'd told Bonnie there was no trouble at the plant, so it couldn't be that. His work was the one thing Mila might allow to take precedence over their relationship. She knew how much that meant to him and to a lot of other people in Rochester. No, his morning commitment was something else, probably a golf game—or another woman. Rick said he had a slew of them. Brett just wanted to talk her into spending the night at his guest suite, with the convenient door adjoining to his own quarters.

She was nothing more than a little variety in his life, and she was glad she'd left the party. That wimp of a Harvey telling her Brett had "had a word with him"— given him an order was what he meant. No wonder Brett's head was as big as the Goodyear blimp, with everybody catering to him. Bonnie was no better, with her careful calls to announce her approach. Mila was sorry she'd let him off so easily. She should have given him a piece of her mind. If she ever saw him again she would. But she wouldn't be seeing him, and that was almost worse than the rest.

Mila lost track of the taxi ride till she saw her hotel spin past the window. "Stop, that's my hotel!" she called to the driver.

"Is that were you're staying? You said 'the hotel.' In Rochester Jack Orr's place isn't 'the hotel.' I'll turn around in the parking lot."

When the taxi stopped, she saw they had entered a one-way street. Rather than drive around the block and pay the extra fare, she decided to get out and just walk around the corner. It was only a few steps. As she turned the corner, she saw Bob's car parked on the other side of the street. He must be looking for her. Vague worries floated through her mind as she hurried to the desk. At least he and Rick weren't racing tonight. Not much could happen to spectators.

"Was someone looking for me?" she asked the clerk. Miss Duntan considered herself quite an intimate acquaintance after a few days' familiarity. She was privy to all Miss Dempster's callers, her comings and goings. The day clerk's recounting of Mr. Fletcher's call, and of the affair at the pool in particular, had brightened her life considerably.

"Why no, Miss Dempster," the clerk said.

"I saw my brother's car outside. I thought maybe he was here."

"Is that the tall, red-haired young man who was in your room earlier?" the clerk asked. This too had been related as newsworthy gossip.

"Yes."

"You'll likely find him and Rick Healey downstairs in the tavern. Rick often drops in on a Saturday night. There aren't many hot spots in Rochester. Our Zanzibar Lounge is where the young crowd hangs out. We serve finger food and drinks. There's no live entertainment this week, but they have one of those deejay fellows down there playing records. Why don't you go down and join them?"

Mila glanced at her watch. It was eleven-fifteen. She knew sleep would be long coming and she also suspected that Brett might call and try to talk her into seeing him. It would serve him right to discover she was out. "Which way is it?" she asked.

"You don't have to go outside at all. You can go down that staircase on the left, and at the end of the hall there's a door. That's the Zanzibar Lounge."

"I'll take a peek and see if my brother's there. Thanks."

As soon as Mila reached the landing halfway down the stairs, she could hear the music coming up from the hall below. By the time she reached the bottom, she could feel it. It was so loud the walls trembled.

One of those places! She wasn't sure her head could take it.

She opened the door into a room of utter garishness. The only affinity with Zanzibar was the fake tiger skins on the seats, and a pair of crossed spears on the red wall. Other than that, it was just a loud bar, with a big dance floor in the center of the room. Disco lights flashed on the dancers, reminding her of the Japanese lanterns at Bonnie's party, but there the similarity ended. This was a rowdier, younger crew, and the music was raunchy rockabilly. Through the strobe lights, she peered into the shadows for Bob and Rick.

Bob was not to be seen, but Rick was at a table, vigorously attacking a basket of potato skins and chicken wings. She went to join him.

"Hi, doll face," he said. "Nice outfit. Who're you trying to impress?"

"Nobody."

"You succeeded," he said, with no intention of giving offense. Quite the opposite, he smiled his appreciation and moved over to make room for her. "You're back early. Was the party a bummer?"

"The pits. Where's Bob?"

"He's dancing," he said, pointing a chicken wing toward the floor.

Mila looked, and recognized that the maniac under the red light, awkwardly gyrating more or less in time to the music, was her brother. His partner might be the small dark-haired woman in the red dress, or possibly the big blonde in jeans. None of the three looked at each other, nor danced close enough for Mila to be sure.

A waiter appeared at her elbow and asked, "What'll you have?"

It was warm in the room. "A draft beer," she said.

"You should've gone to the races," Rick told her.

"I wish I had."

"It was great," he said enthusiastically, and before she could divert him he was off on a description of incredibly short elapsed times, of skids and burnouts and other mishaps that had made the race so worth attending.

She might have heard one word in ten over the music if she'd been really interested, but other matters pressed on her mind. As Rick seemed perfectly happy with a monologue, she let him talk, just nodding and smiling occasionally to satisfy him that he wasn't talking to himself.

The record ended, and Bob came toward the table with the small dark-haired woman and introduced her as Debbie. "Hi. Love your dress," Debbie said to her.

"What're you doing here?" Bob asked his sister.

"I saw your car outside and decided to investigate. I'm just going to finish this beer and go up to my room."

"We have to have a dance first," Rick said.

"I'm too tired to boogie."

"One dance. Come on, Mila. There aren't half-enough girls to go around. I've been in Park ever since we got here. My motor's all revved up to go."

"You're eating."

"Now I'm finished," he said, and stuck the last potato skin into her mouth. "Come on, doll face, put it in gear."

"Okay, but just one dance," she bargained, swallowing the toughest potato skin she'd ever tasted.

"You're the best looking girl here. We'll have an attack on our table once the guys get a look at you," he promised—or maybe it was a threat. The "guys" looked pretty ragged around the edges.

"Love your hairdo," Debbie said, as Mila got up.

"Thank you." She noticed Bob had chosen one of his usual scintillating conversationalists.

The deejay put on an old Elvis record, and Rick began dancing with great enthusiasm. He was probably imagining he was tooling down the highway in his 383 Magnum 'Cuda. Glancing around at the other dancers, Mila saw that she was flagrantly overdressed. She liked dancing, but not in a place like this, in her high-heeled sandals and with her hair up. The Zanzibar Room was casual enough that she just kicked off her shoes and dropped them at the side of the room. It would be the end of her nylons, but suddenly she wanted to dance. Movement was easier now, and soon she began to enjoy it. Her hair didn't stay up for two minutes. It fell over her shoulders and floated free as she circled and swayed to the insinuating rhythm.

It felt good to forget her troubles and let her body shake away all the tension that had been building over the evening. The only problem was that her low-cut dress developed a tendency to slip off one shoulder.

But it was in no danger of actually falling off, so she forgot about it. She closed her eyes and let the music take hold of her. She abandoned herself to its primitive beat, moving sinuously to the twang of guitars and Elvis's plaintive croon. Every one of her senses was on hyperalert. She could even feel the color of the strobe lights through her closed lids. Pulses of red and green and blue beat on her, each tinting her in its own shade. Diabolic red faded to ghostly green, to eerie blue, as she danced like a whirling dervish, and no one on the floor, including Rick, gave her a second look.

That was the best part of it, to abandon yourself in the privacy of a crowd, with no one looking or caring. She opened her eyes occasionally to see that Rick was somewhere in the vicinity, and that she wasn't in danger of colliding with other dancers. The beat was within her, it was so loud she could feel it actually moving in her stomach, and yet she reveled in it. It was a song of broken hearts and broken promises that suited her mood. She was a part of the light and noise and movement. She was alive, and the hurt was in abeyance as long as she surrendered herself to the dance.

Drops of perspiration beaded her brow and trickled down her forehead unheeded. It was a moment out of time, an instant's madness that she had never experienced before, but she needed it now, and she gave herself over to it entirely. When at last the music died down she felt spent, exhausted, as though she'd just run the Boston Marathon. She collapsed against Rick.

He put his arms around her and said, "Let's do another lap. What do you say?"

She looked up at him and smiled groggily. "You've got to be kidding. I'm not sure I can make it to the table."

"Maybe you're right. I'll refuel with another plate of wings. I'm running on empty."

She remembered her shoes, and began looking around the floor for them. They had to be there under the crossed spears, but they weren't. One was wedged against the wall a little farther along, the other finally turned up in the middle of the dance floor. Laughing, she and Rick chased after them and he helped her put them on. She looked up, scanning the room to locate their table, and saw Brett Fletcher standing at the door, staring at her. His arms were crossed in an attitude of watching and waiting. How long had he been there? She knew by his grim face, deathly pale, that he had seen her performance, and by the rigid set of his muscles that he hadn't enjoyed it.

Her first instinctive reaction was from the heart, and it was one of horror and regret. But even as these feelings assailed her, her mind took charge. It was none of his business. She didn't have to account to him for what she did. She clutched Rick's arm and continued the walk toward their table. Brett detached himself from the wall and went to join them.

"If you've finished making a spectacle of yourself, I'd like a minute of your time," he said, through clenched teeth.

She tossed her tousled hair over her shoulders. "You've got exactly sixty seconds."

He took her hand and pulled her toward the door. "My purse!" she objected, and went to grab it from the chair in passing.

"Love your date," Debbie called after her.

The door closed behind them, and they were in the long hall leading to the staircase, back up to the lobby. It wasn't the best place for an argument but at least it was fairly private, and Mila had decided she wouldn't go to Brett's car, and she wouldn't let him into her room. She drew to a stop halfway along the corridor and wrenched her arm free. She turned and glared angrily at him.

Her dishevelled hair and dress robbed her of some dignity, but she held her titian head high. "Thirty of your seconds are gone. If you have something to say to me, better say it fast."

"What I have to say won't take long."

"Good."

His lips were clenched, and frustration blazed in the depths of his dark eyes. "This is a fine way to repay me—"

He never got beyond that unwise opening. "Repay you for what? For wrecking my car? For throwing me in the pool? For offering me a one-night stand at the Fletcher Arms? For accusing me of trying to seduce you into giving Rick a job? Or do you mean for interrupting my date, telling Harvey he wouldn't be seeing me home?"

"Don't let on Harvey is what's bothering you. You meant to dump him anyway. You had obviously arranged to meet Healey here."

"That wouldn't be 'obvious' to any mind but a conniving one like yours. If I were about a half a foot taller and fifty pounds heavier, I *would* repay you for what you've done to me."

"You're twisting everything around." Brett scowled. "I didn't wreck your car on purpose. And whatever my faults, they're no excuse for that exhibition of poor taste I was just subjected to. Flaunting yourself in front of a bunch of ogling bums in this dive."

"Don't you call my brother a bum!" she lashed out. "The only reason you were subjected to my exhibition is because you came trailing after me. I didn't invite you. If I'd wanted to see you, I wouldn't have left the party."

"I should have known what you were up to. Kiss and run—that's your style."

Mila's hands went to her hips in an aggressive pose. Sparks shot from her eyes. "And what's *your* style, Mr. Fletcher? Bed them and run? You may do your trick in classier surroundings, but real class requires more than money. You have your flunkies trained to hop at your bidding, but you don't have *me* on a leash. And for your information, I've had more fun in this dive in fifteen minutes than I had the whole night at that boring old fogies' party at the Clarkes's."

He blinked in surprise at this unexpected attack. "I knew respectability wasn't your long suit, but I thought you could take one night of polite society. Why did you go to the Clarkes's party, if that's the way you felt?''

"I'm not a mind reader. How was I supposed to know it would be so dull? You, on the other hand, apparently knew this bar was a dive. Why are you here?"

"I wanted to discuss our future."

"We have no future. My future involves leaving this town as soon as possible and never coming back. And yours, I'm sure, involves more women than even Bonnie Clarke will be able to tolerate for long. If you want my advice, Mr. Fletcher, marry her. You won't find many women so obliging in the matter of turning a blind eye to your affairs."

"Bonnie is only a friend. This has nothing to do with her. And I don't have 'affairs.' ''

"You're probably right. An affair usually lasts longer than one or two nights. What you have are one-night stands. You're pathetic," she said, and turned to stride down the hall.

She saw in the mirror at the end of the hall that he was coming after her, his face a mask of fury, and she walked faster. Before she reached the door he was there beside her, looking at her in the mirror.

"Look at yourself," he ordered.

She looked at the reflection, and was appalled at what she saw. Her hair looked as though she'd been in a hurricane. Perspiration had marked her face, and her dress was all askew, pulled off at one side. The mirror stopped at her waist, but she suspected her nylons and shoes were in an even worse state. She felt like crying, but as that was unthinkable, she turned and lashed out at Brett.

"If you don't like what you see, why don't you leave? Nobody asked you to come here."

"I'm here because we have to talk."

"Sorry, Mr. Fletcher, your sixty seconds are up." She pulled the door open and ran up the stairs to the lobby.

The night clerk's eyes were large with interest. She knew Mr. Fletcher had been in a temper when she told him Miss Dempster was in the Zanzibar Lounge, but that was nothing to the temper he was in now. Such language! Her cheeks turned pink at hearing it.

What he said when he was alone in his car was even worse. His profane tirade was directed partly at himself. Talking to Harvey had been a mistake. And what the hell had Bonnie said—or done—to give Mila the idea there was anything between them? He hadn't been out with Bonnie in five years, and even then it was only business having to do with buying out her father and buying the house. He did sometimes get an uncomfortable feeling around her that she wanted to mother him, to take charge of his life, but *love*? He shook away such an absurd notion.

Following Mila to the hotel had been a bad idea. He should have waited until the show tomorrow. And what if she didn't go? What if he spent the whole morning arranging everything, and she decided to go home? It wouldn't surprise him. He didn't go back to Bonnie's party at all. He had to be up at five-thirty to go to the airport, and he wanted to be alert, to see that everything was done just right for the show. A lot depended on the show. Everything depended on it now. His whole future hinged on a bloody fender that was more than fifty years old. If it had one scratch or dent ...

In her room, Mila looked in the dresser mirror and sighed wearily. What a disgusting mess! She looked as if she'd been crawling through some dirty cellar on her hands and knees. She mentally compared herself to Bonnie Clarke and shook her head in resignation. It was hopeless. Any good impression she'd made at the party was destroyed. He'd think she wasn't fit to associate with his friends.

But it was never his intention for that to happen. The only associating he had in mind was that one party that he'd invited her to. At least she hadn't disgraced him there. Perhaps she'd embarrassed him, maybe, by running home alone when Harvey told her of the change of plans, but that was hardly a disgrace. What did it matter anyway? She'd be leaving tomorrow. She'd never see Brett Fletcher again.

She undressed and had a cool shower. When she came out she felt chilly, and put on the T-shirt Brett had given her, to wear as a nightie. It came halfway down her thighs and looked quite ridiculous, but its soft warmth was comforting. She needed some comfort to face the long night alone.

Chapter Nine

The next morning slivers of sunlight peeped around the edges of the draperies in Mila's hotel room. She awoke to see the Concours was going to have good weather. For herself, the weather would be the only good thing about the day. She already had a nagging headache and was bone tired after a night of tossing and turning in bed. It was eight o'clock. With luck, she'd be back home in twelve hours, and could start forgetting this wretched trip and the disastrous acquaintance with Brett Fletcher.

She decided to have breakfast before going to Rick's garage to see what he and her brother were doing. If she packed her bag to take downstairs with her, she could check out now and leave the bag at the desk for Bob to pick up later. It would save time after the show when they wanted to make an early start getting back. The blue cotton dress she put on was imbued with so many memories that she knew she'd put it at the back of her closet when she got home. The very sight of it called up her one date with Brett.

That was really what their tumultuous affair amounted to—one date, and half a dozen unpleasant meetings. But Mila knew that one evening would always hold a special place in her memories. It had seemed that night . . . No, she was wrong. Even that date had had a bad outcome. She'd thought he was hurrying off to meet Bonnie, but actually he'd gone to Rick's garage. She'd accused him unjustly that time.

A wistful smile hung on her lips as she folded up Rick's yellow T-shirt. That had really got Brett in an uproar. Then it was time to fold the Fletcher shirt. She'd never wear it again, but she wouldn't throw it out, either. It would be put away like the blue dress, embodying memories too painful to face. The memories washed over her, unbidden—the scene in the garage and the subsequent meeting in the park, accusations hurled wildly at each other. Why couldn't she and Brett act polite and civilized like other people? They were both too volatile. Maybe it was her fault, maybe she cared too much. But he was just as bad. Maybe *he* cared too much, too? And maybe she was making a mountain out of a molehill. She scowled at her treacherous thoughts, that wanted to color him shining white.

Mila folded up the last of these painful memories, the green dress, laden with echoes of Bonnie's party, and the Zanzibar Room. Another disaster. But darn it, the dress was new, and she couldn't abandon all her clothes. Hiding things away in the dark wasn't the way to overcome your problems. What she had to do was get busy and acquire some new and more pleasant memories to obliterate the painful ones.

She looked around, gathering up the last of her belongings. What would she do with that basket of fruit? The basket itself was kind of cute. Mom might like it, and she'd give the fruit to Rick. She closed her suitcase and took one last, long look at the room. Just four innocent walls, but she never wanted to see those four particular ones again.

Mila took her suitcase and the basket of fruit down and left them at the desk. She settled her bill and went to the coffee shop for breakfast. Orange juice was absolutely necessary, and coffee was needed to clear her head, but food of any kind seemed repulsive. She was alone, sipping her coffee, when Bob appeared at the door.

"Hi, Sis. You're up early."

"Hi, Bob. Have you eaten?"

"Yeah, I had coffee and doughnuts at Rick's place."

"That man's going to die of malnutrition. He eats nothing but junk food."

"He eats lots of it, though. Is this all you're having?"

"I'm not hungry. What time do you want to go to the Concours?"

"After lunch, I guess."

"Shall we go down to Rick's garage, or...?"

"No!"

She looked surprised at the violence of his response.

"There's a bunch of drag racers there, kind of a rough crowd. I thought we'd just go for a little drive this morning, take it easy. Have lunch somewhere and go on to the show."

Since when did Bob offer to go for a drive when there were drag racers to talk to? But this morning she hardly noticed. "It'll be a pretty long drive," she pointed out.

"We can go out to the show this morning if you like. Have a look at the cars on exhibition. We'll drive for an hour, then hit the show."

"Okay," she answered listlessly.

"Or if you like, you can have the car and I'll go down to the garage," he added hopefully.

This was more like her brother. "Sure, if you like," she agreed. It was strange it even occurred to Bob that she might feel out of place with a gang of drag racers.

"Why don't you give that teacher you met at the convention last winter a call?" Bob suggested. "Mrs. Turner, wasn't it? The one with twins and a reading program. Maybe you could spend the morning with her."

"I could. I'm interested in her reading program, but on the weekend she's probably busy."

"Give her a call," he urged, feeling guilty at abandoning her.

"All right. I'll pick you up at the garage around one-thirty."

"I'll meet you here."

"For heaven's sake, Bob. I've met drag racers before. They're not Hell's Angels," she said, laughing.

"No, I mean we'll have lunch here in the coffee shop. It's nice," he added, with a flickering glance at the mediocre surroundings.

"Okay, see you at one-thirty. Oh, I was going to give Rick that fruit from my room. Why don't I drive you down and drop it off?"

"No sweat, I'll carry it," he offered. "I mean I'm in a bit of a hurry, and you have to phone Mrs. Turner."

This was more consideration than Mila was used to receiving from her young brother, but as he insisted, they went to the desk and she gave him the fruit basket. "I want the basket for Mom."

"Will do."

He smiled and lounged out of the lobby, the basket of fruit on his arm looking rather incongruous. Mila didn't like to call her friend before nine, and went back to finish her coffee to kill time. At five after nine she phoned Mollie Turner and explained that she was in town and would like to see her if it wasn't inconveniently early.

"Early?" Mollie laughed. "I've been up since seven with the kids. I'd love to see you. I was going to take the twins to the park, but I'll put them in the backyard instead and we'll chat. Come right over." She gave directions to her house and Mila felt grateful for someone to talk to.

The Turners lived in a small bungalow in a new subdivision. Mila drove carefully to avoid the children who played along the street and occasionally darted into the road after a ball or a dog. The Turner twins, just a year and a half old, were too young to be out of the yard yet. Mollie sat on the patio guarding the boys as they played in a sandbox. It seemed strange to see Mollie, whom she'd only met professionally before, in shorts and a T-shirt. Mila had to make a fuss over the children before she settled down with her colleague.

First they talked about the reading program, designed to help problem readers. Mollie was enthusiastic and convinced Mila to give it a try. When this was settled the conversation turned to other topics, but with frequent interruptions from the twins. Tommie got sand in his eyes, and Mollie flew to help him. That was when Mila noticed her friend's T-shirt was one of Brett's.

"Does your husband work for Fletcher?" Mila asked casually when Mollie returned.

"Yes, Tom's one of the lucky ones. It's good steady work, and good pay. Brett Fletcher has in-plant study programs, too, to upgrade the workers. Tom's a foreman now," she added proudly.

"That's nice. Do you know Brett?"

"Oh sure, everybody knows him. The plant is like one big family, a team. This is a Fletcher baseball T-shirt I'm wearing. He gives them to the family as well.

He's very active in town politics, too. He stirred up a ruckus about the teenagers not having any place to go, got a hall built for them. And parks for the smaller kids—all kinds of things. He's a really neat guy."

Mila felt strangely gratified to hear it. "Does he go with anybody?" she asked hesitantly. She didn't like to gossip, especially about Brett, but wanted to learn about his private reputation.

"He goes out with different women, nothing serious, as far as I know."

"How about Bonnie Clarke?"

"How do you know her?" Mollie asked.

"I met her at a party last night. Brett was there."

"How'd you meet all the town big shots in a couple of days?" Mollie asked, but she didn't wait for an answer. "Brett would be there, of course. Bonnie's brother is one of his plant managers. She's been pursuing Brett forever, but without any luck. I don't think she really cares for him. The Clarkes used to be big shots in Rochester, and she just likes the idea of being somebody again. That's just a personal opinion. I never met the lady, but that's what I hear around town. I suppose you're here with Madam X," Mollie continued, and Mila was happy to let the subject of Brett Fletcher drop.

What she'd heard jibed with Brett's statement. He wasn't involved in anything with Bonnie. It was just wishful thinking on Bonnie's part, and her discreet dealings were to prevent ruffling his feathers.

Mollie invited Mila to lunch, but she had to meet Bob, and declined. It was only ten to twelve, so she had time for some private thinking. Mila drove out to Stony Creek Park and walked beside the millpond. The ducks and geese reminded her of the geese at The Lobster Shack. Brett even knew the big duck's name— Esmeralda. He really loved this town. She thought she could love it, too. It was unusual for a small town to have so many amenities, both athletic and cultural. It would be nice living here, becoming a part of the community. She already knew Mollie, so she'd soon make friends in her own profession. What she was thinking about, of course, was being here as Mrs. Brett Fletcher, and she shook the thought away.

But the image of Brett refused to go. It had changed in character, but it was still there inside her head. He couldn't be a scandalous playboy, or Mollie would have heard. She'd been born and bred in Rochester. Mila felt she'd been too hard on him. She'd been wrong in thinking he'd gone running to Bonnie the night he went to the garage to see about her car. But she wasn't wrong about last night. He had arranged that he would drive her home instead of Harvey after she said she wouldn't go with him. Still, she'd given him a pretty good idea how she felt at the gazebo. He had every reason to think she'd like a change of escort. It wasn't Brett's fault if Harvey was a wimp.

But if he was really interested in her, why hadn't he arranged his schedule so they'd have a few hours together today, before she left? He'd tried to arrange time for them to talk last night. What must he have thought, to see her all mussed and dancing like a demon with Rick? He must have been disgusted, but he'd still wanted to talk after that.

She'd bungled her last chance to find out how he really felt. Her heart was heavy as she sat staring at the water with unseeing eyes. She could call him . . . Except he'd already told her he was busy all day. She'd gone chasing after him at the party last night. She was becoming as bad as Bonnie Clarke. Oh, what was the use? He lived one hundred fifty miles away from her home. Too far for him to come to Muskegon for a date. But when she returned to the hotel for lunch, she inquired at the desk whether she'd had any calls. She hadn't.

She pressed her lips into a line. So much for Brett Fletcher. She'd have lunch, go to the blasted show and go home.

At least Bob was in high spirits. "You look all bright eyed and bushy tailed," she said when he entered the coffee shop. "Did you see some good cars?"

"I'll say. I met a guy with a '64 Ford Thunderbolt."

"You mean Thunderbird."

"No, Thunderbolt. A special factory SS-class racer—experimental car. Only about a hundred built. They're practically extinct. She runs a 427 engine. What a killer! Rick's going to swap trannies in her."

"That's nice. I think I'll have the chef's salad," Mila said distractedly.

"You don't sound very interested," Bob said, offended at such meager enthusiasm.

"Oh, I am. Let's drop down and see it before we go to the show."

"No!" he exclaimed.

She looked at him in alarm. "Why not?"

"It's gone. The guy that owns it was just getting an estimate. I've been at the garage all morning. Let's just eat and go on to the Concours."

"Fine."

Mila noticed that Bob's excitement lingered while he ate. She liked cars, too, but didn't quite qualify as a motor head. Mostly she just liked driving the speedy muscle cars. She smiled to see how much pleasure Bob got out of his visit to Rick's. She sometimes feared college would be wasted on him, but he was studying mechanical engineering, and probably he'd do well.

They drove out to Oakland University, where the Concours was held among the sand traps on the golf course at Meadow Brook Hall. A large space was necessary for the one hundred and twenty cars to be displayed. She and Bob got their booklets and toured the cars, drooling over the Duesenbergs and Packards, the wonderful, sporty old convertible Hispano-Suiza Speedster, and the 1910 Stanley Steamer. All the rare antiques were primed and polished to perfection, and roped off to keep the spectators at a distance. It took no more than the chance scraping of a buckle or button to do damage to the old paint on some of these cars. Some owners even went so far as to avoid using water, and they cleaned their cars with dry towels.

Mila felt sad to see Madam X in the brochure with Mrs. Douglas Dempster, Muskegon, Michigan, listed as the owner. It made Mom sound like a stranger—so formal. The brochures had been printed weeks ago, and they wouldn't print a new set just because Madam X wasn't appearing.

Some of the owners were dressed in antique outfits to match the era of their cars. There were men in long dust coats and goggles, women in sweeping gowns and others in short twenties' dresses with cloche hats. One masochist wore a raccoon coat over a striped blazer in the heat of August. He looked roasted alive. There was a joyful carnival atmosphere at the show, shared by everyone but the anxious owners, who hoped to win one of the twenty-five different trophies and prizes. Families roamed the grounds, eating popcorn and ice cream, taking pictures and picking their favorite car. The Dempster family had once come to the Concours when Mr. Dempster was alive. That trip had given him the impetus to do a proper restoration job on Madam X.

"One day we'll come back, Margaret," he had promised his wife, "and take home the blue ribbon." This was the year it should have happened, but fate had intervened. Mila wanted to win that ribbon for Dad. They all wanted to, the whole family.

"Let's go into Meadow Brook Hall and have a look around," Mila suggested, when the heat became uncomfortable. The large half-timbered mansion with its peculiar smokestack chimneys looked cool, set against its backdrop of tall trees. "They have a display of automotive art this year. Some of the original drawings from the styling studios. I'm going to see if they have one of Madam X.''

"I'll hang around out at the refreshment tent. Rick should be here soon," Bob answered.

It was cooler in Meadow Brook Hall. Mila toured a few of the one hundred twenty stately rooms with their carved paneling and sculptured plaster ceilings, and decided that she'd be comfortable with about one tenth as much house, or even one twentieth. What a different time the twenties were, people had actually lived in castles. Today a five-bedroom house was considered large. Her mind flew off to Brett's big brick house. She felt a stab of sorrow that she'd never see the inside. She wondered how he'd arranged it, what kind of furnishings he liked. She really didn't know much about him at all.

To rid herself of these thoughts, she went to the art exhibit. Madam X wasn't pictured, but she toured the other illustrations, keeping an eye on the clock. She didn't want to miss the judging, which began at three.

At ten to three, she went back outside and turned left toward the refreshment tent, with the big red-and-white canvas roof. She had already noticed a few Fletcher T-shirts around the grounds, but the one she stared at now brought her to a halt. There was no mistaking those broad shoulders and that slim, tapering body. If the body hadn't been enough to tell her, the proud set of that dark head left no possibility of doubt. It was Brett, and before she recovered from that shock, a new one was added to it. He was with Bob and Rick, the three of them with their heads together like conspirators. She thought they wouldn't have a word to say to each other.

Her first instinctive response was to run to Brett, but as this was out of the question, she wanted to go back into Meadow Brook Hall and hide. This was ridiculous, childish, cowardly and, most of all, counterproductive. She'd even thought of phoning him, so why did she hesitate to go forward now? Was it because she had rearranged the past to lessen the pain, that she had distributed any blame evenly over them both, and didn't want her memories disturbed? Or was she just afraid he'd be politely distant, showing that the past few days meant little or nothing to him?

Before she came to any conclusions, the men spotted her and beckoned her toward them. She pinned a bright, phony smile on her lips and walked forward, with her knees knocking.

"Hi," she said, turning her artificial smile evenly on them all, even Brett. He looked politely distant. "I see Debbie couldn't make it, Bob."

"She had to work. She might come by later. Want some ice cream?"

They were all eating ice cream cones. "Sure. It's hot out here, isn't it? It's nice and cool in the Hall. I've been touring the exhibition," she chattered inanely.

"What kind do you like?" Brett asked her.

Her mind went perfectly blank. There was more than distant politeness lurking in the depths of those dark eyes. There was close politeness at least. More closeness than politeness, and a dash of something else. Whatever it was, it lent an excited animation to him. "I don't even know what kind of ice cream you like," he said. She heard that "even" with surprise. It held overtones of exasperation, of frustrated wishes, of an interest to know all about her.

She became aware that Bob was shaking his head, which told her she was behaving oddly, to say the least. "She likes chocolate," he told Brett.

"Miracles never cease," Brett said with a smile. "We actually have one taste in common." He turned to the counter and got her a chocolate cone.

"Thanks," she said when he handed it to her. "I see you managed to make it to the show after all."

"I finished up my job a little earlier than I thought I might."

"Have you seen the cars yet?"

"Just a quick glance on the way by."

"Ice cream was the real attraction, was it?" she asked.

He tossed his half-eaten cone in the disposal bin beside the tent and gazed at her. "I think you know what the *real* attraction was, Mila."

She found her eyes frozen on his. Some unreadable but very important message was there. A hush was in the air. She should say something—he'd think she was crazy, staring at him like a statue, but her throat was constricted, and the pounding of her heart left her weak and warm all over.

He smiled softly and said, "Your ice cream's melting."

"Oh." She lifted it to her lips and tried to control the ooze that melted faster than she could eat it in this blazing sun. She felt like a child, licking an ice cream cone at what could be the most important moment of her life. She didn't want to be doing this in front of Brett, and didn't want to throw it away, as he had given it to her.

"Hey, you guys," Rick said, "we better get over to the cars. They're going to start the judging now."

"Shall we go?" Brett asked, and took her arm.

Bob and Rick set a fast pace, while Mila and Brett followed more slowly behind. His fingers closed around her elbow, ostensibly to guide her steps over the uneven grass, but it was his touch that she was aware of.

"You haven't mentioned my new style," Brett said.

"I noticed you're wearing one of your company shirts."

"I notice you're not. But even if you've gone all formal on me, while I switched to jeans to please you, I won't complain. At least you're not announcing your intimacy with Rick today."

A breathlessness overcame her. Was he saying he had actually dressed himself to suit her? "I'm not intimate with Rick!" she exclaimed indignantly.

"I thought about what you said last night," he continued. "I suppose we seemed a pretty dull lot to you, at Bonnie's party."

"No, it was very nice," she said quickly.

"Boring old fogies. Dull," he reminded her. "And the music! I don't think the Clarkes have bought a record in a decade. I only realized when I saw you so euphoric, a free spirit, dancing your heart out at the hotel, how staid and dull I must have seemed to you."

"No, really! I hardly ever go to places like that," she assured him earnestly.

"You should. Whatever insults my jealousy delivered to you last night were totally insincere. My real regret was that it was someone else with you, instead of me."

"I made a spectacle of myself. You said so, and you were right. If my students' parents had seen me, I'd probably have been fired."

"There are spectacles, and there are spectacles," he said forgivingly. "You're talking about an eye-catching public display. The world would be pretty dull without any spectacles, wouldn't it? That's what's been lacking in my life—the joy of spectacles," he said, with a laughing look. "I mean until you entered it, of course. Plenty of spectacles since that fateful night. I never was punched out so well before Rick knocked me in the pool. I can't remember being called a jackass by a woman before, either, now that I think of it. And I know I was never accused of being a crook. A good lesson for my ego. It stands to reason a man would learn a lesson from a teacher."

She looked at him uncertainly. Was it possible he was approving of all the unfortunate matters between them? "I think you'd better ditch that," he said, and took her soggy cone to toss it aside, before handing her a handkerchief to wipe her fingers.

A crowd had gathered around the cars and the judging stand when they reached the sand traps. It was hard for Mila to see over the heads of the taller men. She thought Brett would try to find a place for her, but he stopped and looked at her uncertainly.

"I have to go now," he said.

She felt the bottom fall out of her stomach. "Where?"

"I won't be long. I'll be back before the show's over."

"But where are you going?" she persisted.

"I have to meet someone."

The someone suddenly found him. Bonnie Clarke came rushing up, laughing. "Brett, there you are! I've been looking all over for you," she exclaimed. "Good heavens, what are you going in that outfit?" She spotted Mila, and her smile dwindled. "Oh, hello, Mila. What happened to you last night? You didn't think to say goodbye before leaving our party."

Mila felt like a gauche schoolgirl, being reprimanded for her bad manners. "I had to leave rather suddenly. It was a lovely party."

"You've got something on your dress," Bonnie said, and as Mila glanced down, she law a large splotch of chocolate ice cream, right in the front. Bonnie was dressed in an immaculate white sundress and looked wonderful, as usual.

"We'd better go now, Brett. She's with Harvey. I scouted on ahead to find you," Bonnie said, and with a possessive hand on his arm, she waved to Mila.

"I'll be back. Wait for me," Brett said, and hurried away.

Wait for another kick in the stomach? She didn't think so. If Brett wanted to play games, he'd have to find some other obliging woman. She was through. Why did he bother to apologize, to tell her he was the one at fault, if he only meant to dash off again with Bonnie? That was *one* taste they certainly didn't share.

Mila wanted nothing but to leave the show and go home, but of course Bob wouldn't agree, and it wouldn't be fair to ask him to. She began looking around for him, skirting the edge of the crowd, but all the time she was in a silent rage over Brett.

She spotted Bob's red head without much trouble. He and Rick had managed to nudge their way forward to get a good view. She called and they waved to her. An obliging man in a straw hat let her through the crowd to join her brother. She was busy arranging a story to account for Brett's absence, but no questions were asked.

The judges were introduced, mostly men from the automotive industry—design engineers and retired executives with long experience and distinguished qualifications. They had made a close examination of every car, and marked their forms, basing their judgment on grace and beauty.

The prizes for exotic sports, race and special-interest cars were awarded first, before the judges went on to the real meat of the show, the full classics. Madam X was to have been entered in the American Classic, 1925 through 1932. Mila thought the 1932 black and silver Pierce Arrow convertible sedan would probably win the blue ribbon. Madam X would have had a hard time beating the Pierce Arrow. They were about evenly matched. Her heart was bitter at being robbed of the chance to compete. It was all his fault—Brett Fletcher's. And where was he? What was he doing with Bonnie Clarke at a time like this?

Mila couldn't keep her mind on the awards, but when Madam X's category came up, she roused herself to alertness. The judge awarding the ribbon was a retired Ford advanced-engineering executive with white hair. "It was a hard decision to make," he said. "Many beautifully restored automobiles were shown, and they all deserve honorable mention and our gratitude to the owners, who have given so unstintingly of their time, money and trouble to retain these priceless bits of history. After careful consideration, I announce the winner." He paused a moment for dramatic effect, and when he spoke again, his voice was raised higher. "Madam X, owned by Mrs. Douglas Dempster, of Muskegon, Michigan. Accepting the ribbon on behalf of Mrs. Dempster is her daughter. Will Miss Dempster come forward, please?"

There was a round of clapping and shouts, but Mila didn't hear it. She only heard a buzzing of disbelief in her ears as she stood staring with her mouth open. How was it possible? Madam X wasn't even entered. She turned to Bob in confusion. He and Rick were grinning like a pair of hyenas. "Go on, get up there and claim our award," Bob said, laughing.

"But how...? Surely we didn't win with one fender missing! The Pierce Arrow was perfect!"

"So's Madam X," Rick told her.

She was pushed forward, and with her chocolate-stained dress and her head reeling she went to receive the trophy. The judge handed her a bronze replica of a lion mounted on a marble base, and a blue ribbon. There was a thunderous round of applause.

"The ribbon should be put on the windshield of your car," the judge told her. He pointed to Madam X's place. There, where she had seen only an empty plot of sand a few hours ago, sat a shining, perfectly restored Madam X. The patina of her old paint gleamed richly in the sun, with the raked windshield reflecting a golden glow. Chrome and glass sparkled, as though the car had just been issued from the factory. She felt a miracle had occurred. The impossible dream had been fulfilled, and it could only be through the hand of her deceased father, pulling strings from above.

Some response was expected from her. The hush of the audience and the encouraging smile of the judge showed her her duty. She cleared her throat and tried to speak. Only a childish squeak came out. The crowd laughed sympathetically, and she tried again. Her voice was unsteady but the words were distinguishable. "Thank you for choosing Madam X. I gratefully accept this ribbon on behalf of my mother—and my father. This fulfills a dream . . ." She could say no more. Emotion clogged her throat, and tears dimmed her eyes. Madam X became a shiny, black beautiful blur in the distance. "Thank you all," she mumbled, and the sympathetic judge took over.

"The young lady is overcome," he explained.

The young lady had never felt so bewildered in her life. She was led from the platform and directed to Madam X, to attach the blue ribbon to the windshield, for all the world to see. There was another round of applause, then the attention of the crowd was directed to the next prize. But Bob and Rick had wiggled their way to her side.

"Surprised?" Bob asked, laughing.

"Mystified! How did it happen? Where did this fender come from? Rick, did you put on a repro after all? If the judges find out they'll take back our ribbon."

"It's the genuine article," Rick assured her. "It came in this morning from California by plane."

"We've been working at the garage all morning. That's why I had to keep you away," Bob added.

"Oh, you guys!" She smiled moistly. "You went to all that trouble—and the expense." She hugged them each in turn, while tears washed down her cheeks.

Rick kicked his toe in the sand. "Ah, it was Fletcher's idea," he admitted. "He was the one sent a guy to California trailing after Henderson. He arranged it the night after the accident. He came down to the garage around ten and asked me if I could get the fender put on if he got the chrome bar fixed up. That's why he took the fender—to send to California with his man, to make sure the paint and all that was a perfect match. He didn't even tell me at first, and later he asked me not tell you in case it didn't work out. And if it did, he wanted to surprise you. He got up at five this morning to go to the airport and get the fender.

He's been at the garage all morning with us, arranging to get Madam X cleaned up and delivered here on one of his vans."

"That's what he's been doing all day!" she said. A warm gush of emotion engulfed her.

"My job was to keep you away from the garage this morning, and keep you away from the cars once Madam X was delivered," Bob said. "You helped by deciding to go and look at the art exhibit."

"Where is he? Where's Brett?"

"He'll be back," Rick said mysteriously.

"Here he is now!" Bob said, and pointed to the crowd.

Mila turned and saw Brett pushing his way through the crowd, hurrying. He looked harried and impatient, and beautifully worried, as he fought his way toward her. She blinked away her tears and went to meet him.

Chapter Ten

It was a day of miracles, some of them less pleasant than others. Mila pitched herself into Brett's arms, laughing and crying and still dazed by the onrush of events. He lifted her into the air and swung her around. She looked into his eyes as she slid to the ground in a slow body caress. Just before their lips met, she spotted her mother behind him.

"Mom!" she squealed. "What are you doing here?"

"I was about to ask you the same thing!" her mother replied tartly. "A fine way to be carrying on in public. What will your students think? And where's Bobbie, the lummox? I told him to keep an eye on you."

Mila detached herself from Brett's arms in confusion. "You're supposed to be at Aunt Vera's" was all she could think of to say.

"I was. This fellow—" and she turned to stare suspiciously at Brett "—found out from your brother where I was staying and ordered me to Rochester. In a helicopter," she added, nodding her head significantly at such dashing goings-on. "I felt as if I was flying in an eggbeater."

"There was no airport near the cottage," Brett apologized.

"The nice lady who met me at the airport told me that," Mrs. Dempster said. "A Miss Clarke—she's around here somewhere. Looking at some pictures in an exhibition, I believe."

Brett glanced uneasily at Mila. "I asked Harvey first. He was busy. Bonnie offered...." She just shook her head resignedly.

"Since you brought me here, I assume Madam X is being shown after all. Did we win?" Mrs. Dempster demanded.

"First prize, the blue ribbon!" Mila assured her. "And look at the trophy." She gave her mother the lion statue.

Mrs. Dempster grasped it eagerly, smiling. But the smile dwindled to sorrow as she fondled the crouching lion. "Ah, I wish your dad could've been here," she said. "I'll put this statue beside his picture in the living room."

"It was just the way he would have wanted. I only wish you'd been here," Mila replied, and gave her mother a congratulatory hug.

"Me? I'd pay good money not to have to go up on a stage in front of so many people. I was well out of it. You don't know how I was dreading that ordeal. And did we really win? You said some scoundrel destroyed the fender."

"It was Mr. Fletcher, Mom," Mila said, with an admonishing stare. Brett lowered his brows in mock anger. "I didn't say scoundrel," Mila assured him.

"You said a deal worse as I recall," her mother countered. "Rick told Bobbie he tried to wiggle off without accepting his responsibility. And what am I doing here anyway? 'Get on the helicopter,' I was ordered. 'Come to Rochester immediately. You'll be met at the airport. A matter of the greatest urgency.' I thought you were in the hospital at the very least."

"I'm sorry I didn't make myself clear. I was in a rush when I spoke to you, Mrs. Dempster," Brett explained. "I didn't call you till this morning, after I received the fender and was sure it could be put on in time for Madam X's debut. I thought you'd want to be here."

"Since I am, I might as well have a look at Madam X. A blue ribbon, eh?" she asked, somewhat mollified by Brett's apology.

Brett took one of Mrs. Dempster's arms, Mila the other, and they all went to view Madam X again. Over her mother's head, Mila looked a question at Brett, and he smiled an enigmatic, anticipatory smile. "I thought you said something about Mila being hurt,'' the mother said to Brett.

''Not hurt. I said she needed you. You should be here.''

''What does she need me for, if she's hale and hearty?''

''Something's come up,'' he said, but before he could explain further, Bob and Rick shouted and came hastening forward.

''Congratulations, Mom. You won.'' Bob beamed.

The no-nonsense mother told him she was perfectly aware of that fact, and why was he letting his sister carry on so in public?

''Come and see the car,'' Bob answered. He was used to her brusque way when she'd been frightened out of her wits. She'd soon come around.

The blue ribbon affixed to Madam X's windshield wasn't quite enough to do it. ''Didn't any of you have the wits to take a picture?'' she asked.

''The papers have taken dozens of pictures, Mrs. Dempster,'' Brett said. ''I'll see that you get some.''

''Are you from the newspapers?'' she asked.

''No, actually I have a couple of men lined up who are interested in buying Madam X.''

''Oh, you're after a commission,'' she said. ''I'm not paying any ten percent. I can easily find a buyer myself, with that blue ribbon on the windshield.''

''Mom!'' Mila howled in chagrin.

Brett just shook his head. ''I'm not a salesman,'' he told the lady, ''but I thought you should be here. There's old Colonel Harper from Detroit—he won't offer top dollar. The other is your likelier buyer. Mr. Loomis came for the show especially to see your car, and has to go back to Texas tomorrow. Mila told me you're eager to sell."

"That's the truth," she answered simply. "That car's been a headache to me for twenty years. She was worse competition than another woman. And the expense! Doug left a list a mile long of things I should do to take care of her—moisture-proof room and all kinds of maintenance. I can't devote my life to a car. I'm a working woman. I've got a job. Besides, we need the money. Where's you friend from Texas?"

"He'll be along shortly."

"You got the job!" Mila exclaimed.

"It was a snap. I start Tuesday, so we'd better find Mr. Texas and get this deal settled." She decided Brett was more knowledgeable than her children and sought his advice. "What do you figure I can ask for her, with the blue ribbon?"

"I wouldn't take a penny less than three hundred thousand," he replied. "Ask for a third of a million, and let him bargain you down to three hundred thousand."

Mrs. Dempster just looked at the car and shook her head. "I don't know how many times I called my husband a fool and worse, mooning over this old heap. A third of a million! That Texan must be crazy. Doesn't he know he's just buying trouble?"

"What's life without a few troubles?" Brett asked, his dark eyes flickering toward Mila. "Besides, he likes trouble. He must—he's already got a dozen antique cars. Here's Mr. Loomis now.''

Unfortunately, Mrs. Dempster took exception to Mr. Loomis on sight. He wore a cowboy hat and a jacket with what she considered a very ''funny'' cut to it. He smoked a big smelly cigar and talked too loudly to please her. All these faults might have been overlooked, but she could not overlook being called ''little lady'' when she was at least ten years older than he was.

''Is this the little lady who wants to sell me her car?'' Mr. Loomis asked, sticking his thumbs in the tops of his trousers.

''I own Madam X,'' she allowed.

''I hear you want to sell her.''

''I might consider letting the car go if the price is right,'' she hedged.

''I'll make you a generous offer. A quarter of a million. What do you think of that, little lady?''

''I think your offer stinks worse than your cigar, little man,'' she replied tartly. Mr. Loomis was about six and a half feet tall.

''Mom!'' Mila whispered, pulling her mother's arm.

Mr. Loomis laughed and removed his cigar from between his teeth. He liked a good haggle. ''I might go as high as two seventy-five, if you'd care to deliver her to Texas for me.''

''Mr. Fletcher,'' she said, turning to Brett, ''what time were we supposed to meet Colonel Harper, the *serious* bidder for Madam X?''

Mr. Loomis's blue eyes narrowed dangerously. "Is Harper after Madam X? The old billy goat." He rammed his cigar back in his mouth and got down to serious bargaining. "Three hundred thousand, F.O.B. Rochester."

"The colonel asked me to let him know when you arrived," Brett said to Mrs. Dempster. "He's at the Hall. I'll give him a call now."

"Why don't we just take a walk over and see Colonel Harper instead?" she suggested to Brett, while Mila and Bob exchanged horrified glances.

"Three fifty," Mr. Loomis said. "My best offer. That skinflint of a Harper won't go as high."

Mrs. Dempster laughed, hooked her arm through Brett's and strolled away, but Mila and the others remained behind to pacify Mr. Loomis. "That'll put a good scare into him. Little lady, indeed!" Mrs. Dempster scoffed.

"It's an excellent offer," Brett advised.

"I know it. I did pretty well, didn't I? I'm a businesswoman, you know."

"You did superbly, Mrs. Dempster. I see where your daughter gets her chutzpah."

Colonel Harper was a dignified gentleman. He called Mrs. Dempster "Mrs. Dempster," and haggled much more discreetly, but he admitted his ceiling price was three hundred thousand.

"Loomis offered three fifty," she said.

"I believe you, but Mr. Loomis will put Madam X in his private collection to be seen by only his own friends. All two or three of them," he added testily.

"Three hundred thousand is all I can afford. I plan to put her in my museum, to be available for posterity."

She considered for a long while. "Doug would like that," she said decisively. "He'd want everybody to admire Madam X." She stuck out her hand for a firm shake. "It's a deal, Colonel Harper."

"Excellent. I'll have to contact my bank tomorrow and arrange the funds. Where can I be in touch with you?"

"Mrs. Dempster will be spending the weekend with me," Brett said, and gave his phone number to finalize the details.

"Will I?" she asked, surprised.

After the colonel left, Mrs. Dempster looked at Brett. "The children will think I've gone mad, throwing away fifty thousand dollars."

"Mila will understand."

"I know it. She's an old softy, like me. It's Bobbie I'm thinking of. Never mind. It's none of his business. Three hundred thousand is more than we ever thought we'd get for the car, and more than we need. You know, now that I'm finally getting rid of her, I begin to think I'll miss old Madam X."

"You can always go to Harper's museum and see her. It's only a few miles away, in Detroit."

"It's more than a few miles from Muskegon," she pointed out.

"I hope you'll be coming to visit us, from time to time."

This oblique statement was readily understood by the mother. She lifted an eyebrow and studied the handsome young man beside her. "That's strange. I thought Mila would choose a duller fellow. She usually dates teachers and businessmen. You're in the business of fixing up old cars, are you, Mr. Fletcher?" Her eyes scanned his T-shirt and jeans as she spoke.

"I seem to be dull enough to suit her." He smiled. "No, I never had much to do with old cars before. I'm into metal, though. I do different things with metal," he said vaguely.

She didn't know whether he was a maker of those hideous metal sculptures that ruined the entrance of so many buildings or a collector of scrap metal. But after what she'd seen on the grounds, she knew Mila's mind was made up, and didn't offer any objections.

"We'd better go and find the children," she said. Despite their objections, she never could remember to call her offspring anything but children.

Mila and Bob were already on their way to Meadow Brook Hall and met her at the door. Rick was off admiring other antiques. "We got Mr. Loomis scared up to a possible three seventy-five," Bob said smiling.

"I've already sold Madam X," she said, lifting her chin.

"How much?" Bob asked.

"Three hundred thousand even, and never mind telling me I'm an idiot. I already know it." She explained her reason for taking the lower offer.

"That's what Dad would have wanted. You did the right thing," Mila said.

"Three hundred thousand—that's still pretty good," Bob agreed.

"Since Mr. Fletcher tells me I'm staying at his house, I wouldn't mind going and having a cup of tea," Mrs. Dempster stated.

"You're staying at Brett's?" Mila asked.

"I'll have to stay overnight, I suppose. I've got to settle the deal with Colonel Harper, and I don't intend to fly in a plane after dark. I don't mind sleeping on a sofa," she added to Brett.

"That won't be necessary," he assured her.

"Brett has a guest wing, Mom," Mila explained.

The wary mother feared she'd be subjected to the crashing of metal half the night, but she was curious enough to see her daughter's new home that she didn't renege. "Where are you staying, Mila?"

"I was staying at the hotel. I can probably get my room back." She looked doubtfully to Brett, wondering if he'd invite her to stay with him as well, now that her mother was there to remove any hint of indiscretion.

"There are two bedrooms in the guest wing," he mentioned. "Why don't you all stay there?" His invitation included Bob.

"That's very kind of you," Mrs. Dempster said, tacitly accepting for them all.

"Now shall we go and have that tea?" Brett asked.

Bob wanted to find Rick and tell him they were leaving. Mila went with him as she knew the route to Brett's house, and Mrs. Dempster went with Brett. "Oh my!" she said with a sigh as he drove up the driveway to his impressive mansion. "It's enough to make you think you were back at Meadow Brook

Hall. I didn't realize there was such a good living in scrap metal.''

"I don't deal in scrap metal." He smiled. "I manufacture various items."

She looked around leerily, but saw no revolting specimens of his work. "What kind of items?"

"Automobile parts, surgical instruments, ball bearings."

"I see!" An approving smile lit her face, and she was very careful to say thank-you when he opened her door for her. She did wonder, though, why a successful manufacturer ran around in a cheap-looking T-shirt. Mila would have to smarten him up.

The group all had tea in Brett's living room before the Dempsters were shown to their wing. Mila was happy to see her mother had ceased her unintentional insults. It allowed her to examine the room without fear of trouble breaking out between them. She approved of Brett's taste, good old furnishings that were interesting without being ostentatious, and some more modern artworks and accessories to lighten the air. There were dozens of questions buzzing around in her head, hundreds of things she wanted to say to Brett, but she needed privacy to say them.

That privacy didn't come for several hours. Brett took them all to dinner at the Gatsby Getaway, a glamorous old mansion nearby, with authentic historical furnishings. The house had been turned into a small hotel and dining room. Mila wore her green dress again. Already it was picking up some pleasant memories, to wash away the recent bitter ones.

After dinner Bob had a date with Debbie, and Brett took the women home. Mrs. Dempster decided it was within the bounds of common decency to let Mila join him for a drink in his own part of the house, while she went to her room to make plans for her fortune. Buying out Annie Morin's store was at the top of the list.

The night was so fine that Brett suggested they take their drinks out to the patio. The stone floor was edged with a concréte railing, waist-high, punctuated with pots of flowers. They put their glasses on the table and went to the railing to gaze out at the garden. Moonlight shone on them, bathing the rugged contours of Brett's face and the softer planes of Mila's in pale light. The warm August breeze moved her curls and played along her bare arms, but the shiver that went through her wasn't caused by this mild zephyr. It came from within, from being alone with him, at last.

With all the confusion of things she wanted to say, she hardly knew where to begin. "Why didn't you tell me?" she asked simply.

"Tell you what? That I sent for your mother?"

"About the car. Brett, I feel so awful when I think of the things I said." She shook her head ruefully.

He grabbed her hands and smiled down at her. "You only *said* unkind things. I'm the one who did the harm. When I realized how much the car meant to you, I was sick with remorse. And to add insult to injury, I accused you of trying to gouge me. I scarcely looked at the car in the rain that night. It looked like any old hulk."

"I shouldn't have been driving it. It was stupid of me."

"Let's not try to divide up the stupidity. We'll each take fifty percent of the blame. It was dumb of me to have Harvey bring you to the party, and then..."

"*You* had him bring me!"

"You wouldn't have accepted an invitation from me, would you?"

"I was hoping you'd invite me," she admitted.

"You hid your eagerness very well! That's why Harvey agreed so readily to let me take you home. I didn't order him to, you know. I bend over backwards to keep a good atmosphere at the plant," he said earnestly. "Then when you suggested at the party that we get together the next day, I had to refuse, because I was going to be busy with that other infamous lady, Madam X."

She shook her head. "I'm beginning to realize why Mom was always jealous of her."

"Don't blame the car. It was my fault—a thoughtless moment, driving too fast—and your dreams were shattered."

"Only delayed a year," she pointed out. "But why didn't you tell me you were trying to get the car ready for showing this year?"

"I should have. I had decided to tell you last night when I went chasing after you and found you drowning your sorrow in dance." He stopped a moment and gazed at her, as though mesmerized. "God, you looked beautiful. I knew then I loved you too much to let you go. Why are you smiling?" he asked.

"You just said you love me."

"Surely I've told you before now!"

"No, not quite."

"And you've never come anywhere near it. Do you think you can learn to love a scoundrel?"

"I already have," she said, smiling dreamily.

He lowered his lips for a fierce kiss. His lips moved to the crook of her neck. "I was so jealous when I saw you dancing with Rick last night I nearly creamed him. I hadn't seen that side of you before. I would have hit him, but I needed his help with Madam X the next day."

"He wouldn't have hit back," she said with a laugh. "He wants the chance to work on your transportation. And that is *not* a solicitation!" she added quickly.

"One last apology for that piece of stupidity on my part. When so many apologies are necessary, I begin to realize I'd developed some bad attitudes toward people. A touch of arrogance, no doubt, but you'll take care of that. You were wrong about Bonnie, though. She was delighted to hear of my intentions—about you, I mean."

Mila smiled softly, and kept her own counsel. Bonnie was being her usual discreet self. She'd want to keep on good terms with the Fletchers. She could afford to be generous in her triumph. "It was kind of her to offer to get Mom at the airport."

"And it was only kindness on your part to plead Rick's cause. He approached me about it. I'm letting him have a go at the company cars. He seems to know what he's doing. We'll see how it works out. But for this once, we're not letting Rick Healey interfere with our private business. I kept the repairs to Madam X a secret because I wanted to make up for my mistakes, I wanted to see you look the way you did this afternoon—surprised, happy, delirious enough to say you forgive me. Say you do,'' he urged, and pulled her into his arms.

He held her close against him and her arms went around his neck. She gazed up and read in his glowing eyes a depth of love matched by her own. What had forgiveness to do with anything at a time like this? Or words. She lifted her lips and kissed him, because her heart was too full to speak.

His arms tightened around her, crushing the breath from her lungs while their lips clung together, forgetful of the bumpy road that had led to this happy conclusion.

READERS' COMMENTS ON SILHOUETTE ROMANCES:

"The best time of my day is when I put my children to bed at naptime and sit down to read a Silhouette Romance. Keep up the good work."

P.M.*, Allegan, MI

"I am very fond of the quality of your Silhouette Romances. They are so real. I have tried to read some of the other romances, but I always come back to Silhouette."

C.S., Mechanicsburg, PA

"I feel that Silhouette Books offer a wider choice and/or variety than any of the other romance books available."

R.R., Aberdeen, WA

"I have enjoyed reading Silhouette Romances for many years now. They are light and refreshing. You can always put yourself in the main characters' place, feeling alive and beautiful."

J.M.K., San Antonio, TX

"My boyfriend always teases me about Silhouette Books. He asks me, how's my love life and naturally I say terrific, but I tell him that there is always room for a little more romance from Silhouette."

F.N., Ontario, Canada

*names available on request

COMING NEXT MONTH

CHAMPAGNE GIRL—Diana Palmer
Underneath Catherine's bubbly facade, there was much more to
the champagne girl. But could she leave Matt and her home in
Texas for a job in the bright city lights of New York?

LAUGHTER IN THE RAIN—Debbie Macomber
Although Abby loved Logan, she would still dream about
storybook romance. Tate seemed to walk right out of the pages—
but how long can you hold on to a dream?

THE PAINTED VEIL—Elizabeth Hunter
Thirsa hid her emotions behind her painting. It brought great
artistic success... but left little room for romance. Until
Luis Kirkpatrick. The painter could see her soul—and share her
deepest desires.

HERO IN BLUE—Terri McGraw
Tara was an attorney fighting her first case as public defender.
She was determined not to mix business with pleasure, but
Lieutenant Dan DeAngelo was putting her heart under arrest.

GETTING PHYSICAL—Marie Nicole
Rory had to compete in a minitriathlon to inherit her late uncle's
physical fitness empire. Zak was thrilled to help her train—and
show her the fitness of getting physical... with him!

SWEET MOCKINGBIRD'S CALL—Emilie Richards
More romance among the MacDonald clan, that fun-loving
family you read about in *Sweet Georgia Gal*. Find out what
happens to Wendy and Shane... would their childhood love
endure after seven years?

AVAILABLE NOW:

THE INFAMOUS MADAM X
Joan Smith

LOOKALIKE LOVE
Nancy John

IRISH EYES
Lynnette Morland

DARLING DETECTIVE
Karen Young

TALL, DARK AND HANDSOME
Glenda Sands

STOLEN PROMISE
Christine Flynn

OFFICIAL SWEEPSTAKES INFORMATION

1. **NO PURCHASE NECESSARY.** To enter, complete the official entry/
   order form. Be sure to indicate whether or not you wish to take
   advantage of our subscription offer.

2. Entry blanks have been pre-selected for the prizes offered. Your
   response will be checked to see if you are a winner. In the event that
   these are not claimed, a random drawing will be held from all entries
   received to award not less than $150,000 in prizes. This is in addition
   to any free, surprise or mystery gifts which might be offered. Ver-
   sions of this sweepstakes with different prizes will appear in Torstar
   Ltd. mailings and their affiliates. Winners selected will receive the
   prize offered in their sweepstakes insert.

3. This promotion is being conducted under the supervision of Marden-
   Kane, an independent judging organization. By entering the sweepstakes, each entrant accepts and agrees to be bound by these rules
   and the decisions of the judges which shall be final and binding.
   Odds of winning in the random drawing are dependent upon the total
   number of entries received. Taxes, if any, are the sole responsibility
   of the prize winners. Prizes are non-transferable. All entries must be
   received by August 31, 1986.

4. This sweepstakes package offers:

1, Grand Prize	: Cruise around the world on the QEII	$100,000 total value
4, First Prizes	: Set of matching pearl necklace and earrings	$ 20,000 total value
10, Second Prizes	: Romantic Weekend in Bermuda	$ 15,000 total value
25, Third Prizes	: Designer Luggage	$ 10,000 total value
200, Fourth Prizes	: $25 Gift Certificate	$ 5,000 total value
		$150,000

   Winners may elect to receive the cash equivalent for the prizes offered.

5. This offer is open to residents of the U.S. and Canada, 18 years and
   older, except employees of Torstar Ltd., its affiliates, subsidiaries,
   Marden-Kane and all other agencies and persons connected with con-
   ducting this sweepstakes. All Federal, State and local laws apply. Void
   in the province of Quebec and wherever prohibited or restricted by
   law. Winners will be notified by mail and may be required to execute
   an affidavit of eligibility and release which must be returned within
   14 days after notification. Canadian winners will be required to
   answer a skill testing question. Winners consent to the use of their
   names, photograph and/or likeness for advertising and publicity pur-
   poses in conjunction with this and similar promotions without addi-
   tional compensation. One prize per family or household.

6. For a list of our most current prize winners, send a stamped, self-
   addressed envelope to: WINNERS LIST, c/o Marden-Kane, P.O. Box
   10404, Long Island City, New York 11101.

SSR-A-1